WHEN RAVENS FALL

WRITTEN BY
SAVANNAH JEZOWSKI

DEDICATION

For Aunt JoJo—and Joel

And all those facing dragons before their time

TABLE OF CONTENTS

ACKNOWLEDGEMENTS

I would like to begin by thanking the Lord for giving me sleepless nights, frequent nightmares and an overactive imagination. Without these three things, I would probably be writing about tea and the weather. I would also like to thank Him for my support group. Daddy, thank you for encouraging me to go to college and allowing me to study Creative Writing instead of something practical, like Engineering. Marmee, thank you for believing in my stories and allowing me to hole up in my bedroom for days on end while I played with my imaginary friends. Jess Steingass, thank you for reminding me that I have real friends with real kids who like to eat hot chocolate straight from the can and dump rice on the floor.

I am so grateful for each of my Beta Readers—Tammy, for your boundless enthusiasm; Meredith, for your sweetness and transparency; Rebekah, for asking the hard questions and for brainstorming with me. Nadara Merrill, thank you for the endless hours you devoted to editing this story in spite of your busy schedule and the multiple drafts I sent you. Don Semora, thank you for the gorgeous cover, the formatting and the interior design and illustrations. More importantly, thank you for taking me seriously and answering endless questions. Steve Lake, thank you for introducing me to Don. Anne Elisabeth Stengl, thank you for inspiring me to write for real and not just for myself—thank you for mentoring and giving advice when I needed it most. For all my readers, thank you for allowing me to share a piece of my soul with you. May God give you the courage to face your own dragons, be they small or large, with grace and courage.

Samuel—my dearest one—thank you for loving me, for getting up at three in the morning to brainstorm, for laughing with me when I was excited, for holding me when I was discouraged and for believing in me when I feared no one else did. You are my one true muse.

Joel, thank you for loving squirrels and for inspiring me to write about the hard things.

And, most importantly, dear Aunt Jojo.

Thank you for facing dragons.

When Ravens Fall

"Frigg's Prophecy"

My son is raven cursed,
Slave of bone and fire.
Ice there is,
And empty halls
And a great tree burning.
Swords be broken
Shields be cleft.
Will no one love my son?

~

The raven falls.
Fire freezes and winter burns,
Ashes gather over the Niflheim.
All is lost or not lost
When roses bloom no more.
Ever by blood
Fate is slated.
Will no one love my son?

PROLOGUE

The question hung on the air, charged with risk.

The bone girl waited, her arms held away from her sides, her body stricken with infirmity and disease. She waited because she believed the Gossip was wrong—that the Raven King's son would not be swayed by her disguise—that his feelings for her would prove stronger than appearances.

As the silence stretched out too long, the bone girl repeated her question. "Can you love me like this?" This time her words trembled as her fear began to surface. Still, the young man before her would not speak. He merely stared at her, his expression stricken with horror.

His silence was answer enough.

The bone girl did not need to use tricks to extract the truth from him. She could read it in his eyes and hear it in his silence. He opened his mouth as if to speak, but words failed him even as his hands flexed and then hung limp against his legs.

Around them, raindrops pelted the fortress's courtyard, stinging the stones with their brutality. The bone girl felt it against her head and shoulders just like she felt the fear ripping her open on the inside.

"Is a man's love so frail—" she began, her hands trembling as they stretched toward him.

He recoiled and withdrew further into the shadows. This simple defensive movement sent a shard of pain through her heart. She felt the tears pressing against her eyes, thundering down from the sky. The howls in her head were mirrored in the throes of the storm. The pale Mist began to rise from the ground and curl around her, as if sensing her pain.

The Gossip had spoken the truth after all. The Raven King's son could not even look at her.

"You should go," he whispered.

She opened her mouth, but he jerked his face away from her, one hand slicing the air as if to silence her. "Do not speak to me. You—you've deceived me—you—just go. Please."

When she lingered he whirled to face her—rain on his face, thunder in his voice. "I said, go!"

In that moment it did not matter that her deceit was merely a mask, that the bone girl he claimed to love was truly whole and young and healthy. He did not see the truth in her. He only saw the mask. She stumbled backward, to the ground, the rough stones digging into her palms. She scrambled away from him, ripping the hem of her skirt as she found her footing. Something clenched the bone girl's heart as she turned and plunged into the storm. He had turned her away. He had promised forever and meant something else.

He had betrayed *her.*

She felt the Mist surging up around her, a thundercloud about to explode. She let it build, let it fill her with righteous anger and unbridled hurt. The pressure inside her was so strong she knew it would kill her if not released. Something moved in the Mist. The bone girl pulled up short as a woman appeared in the swirling shadows.

It was the mother, Frigg. The woman peered at her from beneath the hood of her cloak, her face mottled with shadows. "You are not meant for him," she whispered. "You will bring him to ruin if you do not give him up. I have seen it."

The bone girl bit down on her lip, the physical pain a mirror of her inner hurt. It was the other way around. He had given her up, because looks meant more to him than she did.

"Give him up," Frigg repeated, but her voice began to sound far away.

The Mist and the darkness closed in on the girl. The pain was simply too much to endure. If she did not let it free, it would claw its way out of her. Already she could feel it roiling against her insides as if it were

2

a living thing. The Mist writhed around her and began to take shapes she had not asked it to. She could not control it.

She cried out, her voice frail against the night. Something was wrong. She collapsed to her knees and clutched her midsection as the storm surged in intensity. The lashing rain seemed to taunt her.

Let him go, let him go, let him go.

The bone girl could not move. She could barely keep her eyes open. Around her, the thunder was replaced by screams. She felt tremors begin in her fingers, tremors that spread until there was no part of her that was not twitching. Her body caved in on itself, her arms spread and thinned into wings and her skin splintered into black feathers. When it ended she lay on the ground, a crumpled black bird.

She was girl no more but a raven. Her beak parted, her voice gone, lost in a shrill squawk. Around her the fortress shook with cries of terror.

What had she done?

ONE

A red squirrel scampered through the sprawling village of Sandfell, over frozen woodpiles and around clomping feet wrapped in furs. Although nestled deep in the Ironwood Forest, Sandfell still had its share of visitors. Today was like any other choosing day, the village swarming with local farmers, hunters and traveling hawkers.

The Trials always drew a crowd, even if Sandfell of itself did not.

The squirrel dodged the small clusters of humans although he did not go out of his way to avoid them. Ratatosk visited the village frequently to catch up on the local gossip. People did not frighten him. They told such wonderful stories.

As a shadow slanted across the ground, Tosk glanced up to make sure it was still the raven. The bird angled westward toward the village outskirts and Tosk followed. He bounded past the great house, but paused when a girl with long, untidy hair tumbled out the door and nearly trampled him. He bawled at the girl and dodged her careless feet, but the wench had not even seen him. She flung herself back toward the longhouse as the thick wooden door slammed in her face. She pounded on the door, shouting, but only laughter answered her outrage. Tosk could hear revelry from within—the bellowing of deep voices and pounding of drunken footsteps. The cloying scent of mead and ale and the even less pleasant stench of unwashed bodies tickled his nostrils. Tosk backed away, wrinkling his nose. The warriors' celebration was already well under way even though the Trials had not yet begun.

A girl still needed choosing.

"Very well!" the evicted wench hollered as she backed away from the door. "Be it on your own head!"

Tosk opened his mouth to give her a fierce scolding, but when she turned, her narrow face thunderous as a stormy sky and eyes welled up as if heavy with rain, he changed his mind. He knew this girl—a pinch-faced lass who caused trouble wherever she went. She had scoldings enough already.

Besides, she was not worth his time.

The girl still had not even seen him. Now that she had determined she would not be readmitted to the great house, she stormed away from the wooden structure. "May you slip in your own vomit," she muttered as she passed by him, kicking at the snow as if it were to blame for her troubles.

Tosk resumed his journey, frustrated she had wasted his time on such a day as this. He hurried in the direction the raven had gone, around the great house and the other longhouses where the notable citizens of Sandfell lived and out toward the spattering of lilting huts dedicated to the thralls and outcasts. The girls were already huddled together in the snow, faces pale and tight with worry. Tosk afforded them naught but a glance.

He did not care which one got chosen. Nobody did, until the girl failed the Trials and returned home—then everyone cared. They cared so much they ostracized the disgraced one for her short comings and made sure everyone knew to steer clear of her.

The life of a thrall was hardly pleasant, but the lot of the chosen ones was even worse.

The raven was nowhere in sight when Tosk finally reached the bone woman's hut. He wormed his way under hides strapped over a wooden frame until his face and torso were inside the hut, although he left his bushy tail out in the snow in case he needed to make a hasty retreat. The only thing nastier than the raven's temper was her razor sharp beak. The bone woman, too, was a force to be reckoned with. Tosk knew her secret and had no intention of falling afoul of her good graces.

Besides, he had every right to be here.

If it had not been for him, there would be no need for the Trials in the first place.

Astrid stormed away from the longhouse, her gait long and sure. It should not have surprised her that her father would banish her from his presence, not when she was there to interfere with his revelry. Strong drink did not deal kindly with him, but as he was well aware of the consequences, she could do nothing to help him if he would not help himself.

It did not surprise her that today—of all days—he would be inclined to strong drinking.

Sigurd drank for two reasons: to celebrate his good moods and to drown his foul ones. Often the two seemed to happen simultaneously. Astrid could never seem to predict which mood ensnared her father more deeply, a fault which caused her no end of grief.

It had always been like this ever since she could remember.

Her mother claimed he had not always been this way, but that had been before Astrid's time—before her mother's time, before the dragon.

Astrid plowed through a snowbank, the mere thought of the dragon scorching her on the inside. It might seem odd to some that her life would be so marred by an event that had transpired before she even existed and that she could feel so much hate for a creature she had never seen with her own two eyes.

But Sigurd had seen the dragon, and that sight left scars that battled on even from the confines of the past.

Her face tingled and felt hot. Astrid ducked her face and moved a gloved hand to cover the afflicted area. Her face always hurt whenever she quarreled with her father, as if the scars were evidence of the pain she felt within.

She remembered every detail about the day she received those scars. For a moment—a blissful moment—she had been proud of them. It had been a glorious day, the sort the warriors would speak of in their revelries. Had Astrid been a man she might have joined the warriors in their story telling this day, remembering her first victory and her first scar.

She had been only twelve years old, on her first hunt. The sky had been low cast, shrouded in heavy clouds hovering just above the peaks of the trees. Astrid could still remember the smell of the damp air, charged with power from the building storm, just as she could still feel the warmth of a steady rain as it broke from the sky above her and poured its tears into the forest.

Lightning split the early morning sky moments before the resounding echo of thunder shattered the stillness of the forest. The stag moved out from behind a small stand of scrub trees, startled by the vehemence of the storm.

Astrid felt her heart begin to pound in her chest. The elm bow she held in her hands felt suddenly heavy and cumbersome. Her father had refused to make her bow from yew, not wanting to waste precious wood on a girl child who should not even be joining the hunt. As Sigurd had no son, he had consented to train Astrid with the understanding she would keep meat over the fire so that he could devote his time to other, more profitable things. Astrid's ambitions extended beyond cook fires, but she knew when to bide her time.

This was not a moment to bide one's time. This was a moment to act.

She lifted the bow before her body, fitting the notched arrow against the sinew string. Her muscles trembled as she pulled back the arrow. She had been training her arms to pull the bow for months. Although her bow was small, and she did not possess the strength of the warriors, the stag was only a couple dozen yards away from her. She released the arrow just moments before another shard of lightening jagged across the sky. The stag recoiled into the stand of trees. Astrid could hear it floundering in the brush as she raced after it, her deerskin boots slipping on the sodden grass.

She found the stag lying behind a juniper tree. A grin pulled at her cheeks as she approached. She could not believe her good fortune—her first hunt and her first kill. Surely her father would be proud of her feat here today. She circled around the stag and hurried forward.

In her enthusiasm, she did not see the sides of the stag rising and falling with ragged breaths. She did not see the danger present until the animal recoiled in agony and fright, lashing out with his deadly hooves. The blow to her face sent her reeling backward. It felt as if someone had smashed her over the head with a smithy's hammer. She floundered in the wet grass but came back to her feet, wobbly and woozy. Retching, Astrid hunched over her knees and coughed up blood and teeth.

"Here, girl!" Her father eased out of a stand of trees as if born from the shadows themselves. Astrid stumbled toward him, obedient but nearly blind with pain. She bit back the sobs clawing at her throat and focused on her father's angry face.

"That is not the way to do it!" he bellowed at her. He came up behind the stag and pressed a foot against the animal's neck, pinning its head to the ground. There was something fearful about him then. It was not his massive build nor his dark, swarthy face fringed in untamed snarls of hair.

Her father had the look of death in his eyes.

Astrid found herself in awe of its power. Sigurd thrust a blade into her hand and shoved her in front of him. "Never underestimate your prey," he said in her ear as he grabbed her hand and shoved her down toward the stag's head. Astrid wanted to recoil from the large rack of antlers mere inches from her face, but she let her father guide her trembling hand toward the animal's throat. Blood ran from her face and plopped against the stag's trembling nose. With Sigurd's hand guiding hers, the blade slipped into the poor beast's throat and wrenched it open, side to side, in one swift motion. Blood poured over their intertwined hands. The stag's blood was hot and smelly, but Astrid did not care.

The stag was dead. The kill was hers.

She twisted to look up at her father, victorious. But Sigurd grabbed her face so that he could see her injury and released her roughly, the sudden motion sending spasms of pain into her head, peels that echoed the thunder in the sky above them.

"Now you've done it," he muttered as he shook his head side to side. "It's well you can shoot: No man will wish to wed a face like that."

With those few words, he had managed to turn her proudest moment into her weakest. She would never forget it. Astrid's hand moved over the old scars, remembering the days of agony that followed, and the months of ridicule after that. Her tongue snaked across her mouth to the gap in her teeth, where two missing molars had once belonged, yet another reminder of everything she had lost that day.

The sky opened once again, but instead of rain it loosed a flurry of thick snowflakes. Astrid looked up at them without breaking her stride, blinking as the flakes settled on her lashes. It was a bitter day for the Trials, but most suitable. Her gaze shifted from the white sky to the huts springing up around her. She had left behind the boxy longhouses and now moved past lopsided huts strung with thatch and pelts. Ahead of her, she could see a jagged line of eligible girls huddled around the bone woman's hut.

She moved close enough to hear their conversations. They were afraid, and well they should be. The Trials were kind to no one. Life, in general, was not kind to women. Astrid's teeth ground together as she paused to stare at the thralls, their faces pale as the snow drifting around them.

The bone woman appeared with a clay bowl in her knobby hands. One by the one, the thralls moved to drop their offerings into the bowl, bits of animal bone or clay pottery etched with a distinguishing rune to mark it as their own. Astrid removed her glove and reached into her pocket to finger the bit of bone she always carried with her. She had been six years old when she first became aware of the Trials and did not understand then that she would never be called to join the line of girls. She had pilfered a shard of bone from a wild boar killed by her father's hand and had worked it smooth, carving it with a rune to claim it as her own. It was only later she discovered the daughter of a dragon slayer was above such things, although she doubted Sigurd would care one way or the other if she were to suddenly disappear into the snow, an offering to appease a beast in search of a suitable wife.

It seemed the cursed one had unusually picky tastes in women. Hundreds of girls had gone to him, only to be sent home disgraced and unloved.

The bone felt warm and smooth and familiar against her fingers. Once again she felt the desire to cast her lot with the thralls, to stand a chance of bringing honor to her family. There were whispers of the treasures that would descend on Sandfell if the village succeeded in breaking the curse, but that wealth had remained as elusive as the wind. Astrid's longings were hopeless ones, she knew, because she could never succeed with the Trials, even if she were to be chosen. Astrid had no interest in vying for the affections of the cursed one, no matter the prestige and wealth he could bring her family.

Something stirred behind her. She turned to see a gaunt face peering out at her from the safety of the hut. It was Tyra, her eyes haunted by more than shadows. Of course, this girl would watch today's proceedings with more than casual interest.

Tyra had been the last Trial, returning after only a fortnight, left at the village boundaries by the raven to endure the shame of her failure. No one would wish to wed her now. Her life would be one of neglect and shame. They said she still woke crying from the night terrors.

Astrid turned away from the girl's pain, her own emotions rising up inside like a fist trying to choke her. It had always angered her that the lives of the innocent meant nothing, that they could be ripped from their homes and sent out into the cold to keep house for a monster who cared as little for them as a dog cared for the fleas on its back.

Surely there was a way they could all be free from this bitter tradition. But it was clear after fifteen years that no man would ever fight for them. No one would risk being branded a coward for trying to keep his daughter at home. No, the girls were on their own.

Astrid exhaled, the heat of her breath fogging the winter air, the seed of a thought sprouting deep inside her and blooming like a flower in the spring. It was a reckless idea, but one too strong to ignore.

Perhaps a man could not fight for them, but maybe a woman could.

TWO

The raven who watched the bone woman was thin, angular and as sleek as a seal's back arching out of cold waters. She hunched into herself, perched on the hag's shoulder, leaning to one side to peer around a snarl of untidy white hair. The bone woman shook a clay pot filled with the bones. When she smiled, her lips parted to reveal blackened stubs where teeth had once been.

"It is time, bird," the bone woman said, cackling.

Kenna ruffled her feathers and once again became still. It seemed a lifetime ago when the bone woman took Kenna under her tutelage, teaching her to understand the secrets of the Mist. Perhaps a lifetime had already passed. She did not know. She no longer reckoned time the way most people did.

She was a creature out of place and time. Once she had imagined she belonged, but then she took the advice of a fool and became one herself. Were it not for the vow she had taken to see the Trials to the end, she would belong nowhere. She had no family or friends, no place to call home.

The bone woman was as much kin to her as anyone.

Only yesterday Kenna had heard the doleful toll of the bell. The Trials began again. And, like so many times before, she had come to watch. The Mist came and filled the hut with its damp presence. Kenna closed her eyes as she waited for the Sight to take her and for its secrets to be revealed. When it came to visions and healing, Kenna had never excelled. It seemed her talents were for causing trouble, not keeping it at bay.

When the Mist finally came, her companion sighed, and they both opened their eyes.

Silence reigned in the first light of the frozen dawn. Nothing stirred. The naked limbs of the trees became visible, nestled under shrouds of snow. Even the river's voice was uncharacteristically muted with stillness and deep dread.

Then Kenna felt it.

The first hint of a breeze ruffled her feathers and stirred the oppressive silence. The Trials would begin again.

The bones were choosing.

A stronger breeze lifted, from over the river. Fog swirled above the banks. For a moment there was a form in the fog. A girl stood aloft on a wooden deck, dressed too well for a thrall. Her red-gold hair had been braided with painstaking care, in an arduous and time-honored tradition. She stood undaunted against the unknown, spine as straight as a warrior's lance.

Kenna hated her instantly.

Beside the girl, a dragon head appeared, its hide scaly and hideous and its maw open in eternal hunger. Still, the girl never stirred or even shifted her gaze from the Mist. The dragon turned so that a gleaming eye stared right at Kenna. She felt the old terror rearing up inside her, but then the dragon stilled, solidifying until it became nothing more than the bulkhead of a longboat.

The raven dared to move closer to inspect the girl. If she were the chosen one, the Mist would give them a name. But as Kenna swooped down to land on the harmless bulkhead, the girl with the red-gold hair turned to look straight at her, except she was only half girl, half skeleton.

She smiled at Kenna, the horrible grimace of the half dead. Kenna reared back, her beak parted in a soundless shriek.

Then the girl, the boat and the Mist were gone.

"What does it mean?" the bone woman mumbled as her gnarled fingers snatched up the bones. She shoved them back into the clay bowl and shook it violently, only to spill them out once again. Nothing happened.

Kenna shuddered with a cold borne of more than Skadi's frost. The bones had been cast among the thralls, and yet none had been chosen. Outside, the eligible maidens were lined up, clinging to each other in fear. Always the Mist gave them a name.

Never had the name eluded them. What did it mean?

The flap of the tent was shoved aside. They jumped as one. A girl forced her way uninvited into the hut. Kenna tumbled from the bone woman's shoulder and scuttled back into the darkness, hissing.

It was a girl with untidy, red-gold hair.

The bone woman rocked back and forth, muttering and staring at the brazen wench. Kenna shoved her terror down and forced herself to move closer. The girl glanced her way, revealing the right side of her face where jagged scars twisted her flesh.

This was the girl Kenna had seen on the longboat.

Why would she come to them like this? Unbidden? Uninvited? Unchosen?

The girl glared at them, her chin jutted toward the ceiling as if daring them to cast her out. "I wish to cast my lot with the others," she said and held out a hand. Her calloused fingers held a bit of bone etched with a rune to mark it as her own. "If I volunteer, it should not matter if I am the daughter of a slave or a dragon slayer."

"The bones have already been cast," the bone woman said but took the bone from the girl anyway. She rolled it between her fingers, her face upturned as she studied the volunteer. The bone woman paused and held out the bone for Kenna to see.

It bore the dragon rune.

"The bones chose no one," Kenna hissed, even though she knew the human girl would not understand her. Her old companion would.

"Yes," the woman agreed. "The bones chose no one."

The girl with the scarred face and red-gold hair stood even straighter, as if justified. "Perhaps the time for choosing is at an end," she said through her teeth. She moved her scornful gaze to include Kenna. "It has done us *such* good to present."

"You are not a thrall," the bone woman argued, the bones forgotten at her feet.

For the first time, the girl's dismissive demeanor shifted and pain twisted her scarred face. "Perhaps not," she conceded in a softer tone. "But I am slave to circumstances I cannot change. To be unwanted is a curse of its own. Perhaps the curse will be satisfied with this much."

The girl, however brazen, spoke logic. To this point, the Trials had been a complete failure. No slave girl had been able to love and be loved by Odin's youngest son, and thus the Trials continued. But, then, no slave girl had wanted to be chosen. Perhaps this was a sign that something had changed. Maybe this girl would be the one.

Kenna hissed and rocked back and forth as an unfamiliar emotion began to clamor for attention deep within her hardened heart. Hope beat against her, a fledgling trying to break free of its shell.

Maybe this girl would be the last Trial. Maybe this time Fate would spin a tale of a different sort of fabric.

And—just maybe—all would not end in fire.

THREE

Astrid longed for the warmth of a fire and a bed of pelts in which to lose herself.

The afternoon was brittle, the air almost painful to inhale as her lungs protested every breath. Due to the milder temperatures of the previous day and the sharper temperatures of the night, the top layer of snow had become crunchy like ice. It would have been a small thing had Astrid not slipped on an icy rock hidden just beneath the crust of snow and snapped one of her snow shoes in half. The mangled footwear was at that very moment slung across her back. She resorted to plunging and staggering for every step.

Jar Rann was no small jaunt from Sandfell. Had it been summer Astrid could have ridden a longboat down the river and arrived at the fortress timely and well rested. As it was, she must hike the distance through the woods—alone—because no one else wished to step foot inside the cursed fortress.

"If you hadn't been so clumsy, this would not be taking us *so* long."

Astrid grimaced. The breathy, annoying voice reminded her that she was not quite alone. The talking squirrel scampered ahead of her, his small paws dancing across the hard snow with ease, his body brilliant red against the whiteness. He flicked his tail as he ran and paused frequently to look back at her, to make sure she was keeping up. He chittered as only squirrels can, but somehow she understood him and was not the better for it.

"I said, you should not have been so clumsy," Tosk continued, louder. His nose twitched as he sat looking back at her.

"I heard you," she muttered.

After the meeting in the bone woman's hut three days ago, the squirrel had taken a fiendish liking to her. He dogged her steps like a wolf prowling after a wounded deer. Many of the villagers found the talking squirrel to be a novelty, but she found him to be a dratted nuisance. She would give her own left foot if some clever person were to make him a pint-sized muzzle.

"It is polite to reply when someone speaks to you," the squirrel scolded, clearly annoyed.

Astrid looked to the snow before her feet and struggled a few more steps before answering. "A question merits an answer. Did you ask a question?"

Tosk sniffed.

"If you are so impatient, you are free to continue ahead without me and announce my arrival," Astrid continued, brusquely. "I have no desire to keep you here."

The squirrel's ears stiffened into tense points as he considered her barbed proposal. "That is a splendid idea!" he finally chirped, perhaps unaware of the barb. "Perhaps I shall."

She concealed a smile as relief blossomed within her. "You do that."

His sleek back arched up and down as he scampered ahead of her and disappeared into the trees. At least she might have a few precious moments of solitude before she arrived at Jar Rann. The fortress must not be much further. She could already see the top of the tower rising above the barren trees.

Everything she had ever known was about to change. Her heart thrilled with the prospect of the unknown. She did not know what waited for her there, but she did not fear it. There were many things she feared, but a new life was not one of them.

Baldur had dreamed again of the dragon.

The brown bear hunkered over an oaken desk that would have been enormous for a man, but seemed a child's toy to him. Before him, calfskin paper sprawled across the table. A goose quill and jar of berry ink waited near a paw too cumbersome to wield them. Baldur closed his eyes, tucked his chin to his chest and exhaled. His breath frosted on the air, despite the fire smoldering in the hearth behind him.

His mother's nightmares had slowly become his own. It had often bothered him that his poor mother would foresee his future while he did not, but one could not control what was revealed to him and when.

There were many things he wished he had known earlier.

A stormy night filled with terror clouded his thoughts. Not a day went by that he did not regret that evening, when he did not replay the events from every possible angle, imagining what he could have done differently. But it did him little good; all the regrets in the world could not unweave the strands of history, although many had perhaps tried. The past could not be rewritten any easier than the future could avoid being written altogether.

Time, be it past or future, was a relentless predator.

Baldur opened his eyes and sighed. The sound rattled from his chest, yet another reminder of what he was, and of what he was not. He looked again at the papers before him. The dreams were there, bottled up inside him like a volcano fit to bursting, but he could not pen them. They were caged within him, never to be spoken, never to be written, never to be told.

He could still remember the sound of his quill scratching against the rough paper, could still see the blue-black ink staining the vellum as his thoughts melded into words. There were so many things he wished to say, so many regrets he wished to confess, and so many apologies he wished he could offer.

He regretted his selfish indignity of that night with every waking breath. He had felt himself injured and betrayed. It was only later, much later, that he realized who had truly been injured that night. He deserved the fate that befell him.

And yet, even after all this time, they still had never mended the hurt between them. It was as raw as a putrid wound, festering. It seemed that some bridges were not meant to be rebuilt.

A flutter of wings announced her arrival.

He sighed again. "Odin's Eye, I am in no mood to argue," he growled, breaking the silence he had kept for most of the day. The raven cawed at him; the harsh sound grated on his nerves. There was no telling what she wanted, without Ratatosk here to translate. He could talk until his mouth went dry, but she would not understand his chuffs and growls.

The raven warbled again, more insistent. Baldur turned to look at her. She sat on the far side of the window bench, hunched against the cold. She studiously ignored the potted rose bush dwindling beside her. Instead, she speared him with one glinting eye and squawked a command.

Kenna fluttered over to land on his right shoulder. Baldur cringed and longed to shoo her away, but the talons dug into his fur, anchoring in. When the bird hissed into his ear, he growled and snapped his teeth at her.

He steeled himself for the cacophony that would follow, and Kenna did not disappoint. She cawed and flapped her wings against his muzzle, fluttering down to the desk where she paced back and forth in a flurry of agitation, her blue-black wings lifted around her head as she ranted. He let her have her say; the exact words might have been a little hazy, but her meaning was quite clear.

She did not think he was trying hard enough.

She never let him rest, not for a day.

He was so tired of their quest. They never lasted, these girls, even the bravest of them. There was always something wrong—too shy, too afraid, too blunt or too selfish. He always knew from their first encounter that they were not going to work. Everything that came after was just flair added to the tragedy to make it an interesting tale.

If he still had the ability to write, he would have a collection of ridiculous ballads that would leave the world rolling in helpless laughter. As it was, only he was able to appreciate the spectacle. And he did not find the spectacle humorous.

The raven finished her tirade with a helpless shriek, her wings hitched and partially outspread. She was at once terrifying and ridiculous. Baldur bared his teeth. It was the closest thing to a smile a bear was capable of.

She hissed, and he swiped an offhanded paw at her to clear her from his desk. She fluttered back to the window, twisting her neck around to give him one last furious squawk before she launched into the air.

The bear moved to the window and watched her go, admiring the way the late afternoon sun shone on her glossy back as she fluttered down to the roof top below him. There, she sat preening in indignation, a splash of ink against the crusty snow. Baldur watched until the raven soothed her ruffled dignity and disappeared into the sky.

It took some time.

He studied the view through his window, from the barren ash tree in the courtyard, to the crumbling walls beyond it, and lastly to the forest sweeping down and away from the hilltop fortress. Something stirred in the ash tree, snagging his attention back. He could see a small black shadow in the tree. After a moment, he found the other one, higher up in the skeletal branches.

They were watching him. They were always watching him.

The Raven King may seem to have forgotten about his youngest son, but it was apparent to anyone with eyes that Odin had not forgotten him completely, not when he sent his spies to watch over him with such unsettling frequency.

Baldur growled at the tree before he returned to the pile of pelts in the corner and threw himself down, his eyes buried beneath one paw. He shifted his other paw so that he could stuff it into his mouth and gnaw on it, kneading the leathery pads with his teeth. For some reason, this odd action always comforted him. Perhaps he was like an infant sucking on his thumb, but right now he did not care.

Outside, he heard excited shouts. Tosk had returned from the village, most likely to announce the arrival of the newest Trial. The weight returned to his chest. He struggled to summon some sort of enthusiasm, but the only emotions he felt with any sort of clarity were unease and weariness. They were running out of time and they both knew it. He turned his head and peered from beneath the weight of his paw, eyes on Frigg's rose bush. It had been her parting gift to him, to warn of the times—of the dark times and of the end times.

His mother also dreamed dreams. And she had dreamed of this one long, long ago.

When roses bloom no more.

The rose bush was dying.

This suggested Frigg's most dreaded prophecy was about to come true. It was too soon. There was still so much that he did not understand. He was not yet resigned to his death.

Why did he dream of dragons when it was a raven who haunted his every waking thought?

FOUR

Tosk did his best to prepare a proper reception for the dragon girl, but Baldur and Kenna had never been much for fanfare. Baldur, quite reluctantly, had finally left his tower and now huddled against the cold, his brutish body seeming somehow fragile against the falling darkness. Kenna sulked somewhere, not deigning to grace them with her presence. At least the Watchers seemed to be interested. The brothers were Odin's eyes and ears, roaming the Niflheim to gather news before they returned to the far north to report. Tosk had always felt a kinship to them although they had never offered much up in the way of conversation.

New recognized news, in whatever form it happened to arrive.

The Watchers fluttered down from their perch in the tree to watch from the palisade wall. Munin hissed softly to his brother, but Hugin silenced him with a sharp squawk. Tosk rolled his eyes. As always, Odin's servants were proving to be as unsociable as Kenna. Either Odin had very low standards when it came to his servants or decent volunteers were in short supply, because ravens never ceased to amaze him with their terrible social skills.

Tosk tugged at one of his ear tufts as the dragon girl labored out of the forest and began to make her way up the incline toward the fortress. He felt a thrill sweep through his small body as he wondered if this girl would be the one. She was as unpleasant as the rest of Jar Rann's inhabitants. Surely that was a sign, if nothing else was.

Not that he cared too much one way or the other. After all, none of this was his fault. Exactly.

He had played a very small part, in the beginning. Lovers always played games, so he had thought it would be fun to pit the two young lovers against one another, to test their mettle. When he suggested Kenna test Baldur before throwing her heart away like a silly child, he could not have predicted how *badly* she would play the game, how she would overreact!

He sniffed and flicked his tail. He should have known better because Kenna seemed to do everything badly. He would not blame himself because the raven had somehow cursed the lovebirds and put them all in this terrible mess. Tosk had hung around for the simple fact he knew they would never get out of trouble without him.

He felt abruptly squeamish, but he shoved that unpleasantness away into a dark corner of his thoughts.

Astrid slowed to a halt a few feet from the entrance to the fortress courtyard. Baldur rose up from his haunches to greet her, his nose lifted into the air and quivering as he tested the smell of her. Tosk leaned forward to watch, his breath caught and held in the back of his throat. It felt as if the whole world had stopped to watch and listen.

The girl and the beast observed one another in silence, heads cocked to the side, eyes probing. At last, the girl held out a steady hand to hover mere inches in front of the Baldur's nose. He leaned forward to sniff it. "Hello," the dragon girl said, stiffly. She inclined her head in a show of deference. "My name is Astrid, daughter of Sigurd the Dragon Slayer."

Baldur chuffed once, softly. Tosk leapt forward to translate. "The esteemed son of Odin bids you welcome," he enthused, "and he hopes that you will be happy and comfortable in his home and that this will be the beginning of an unparalleled friendship." He waited, beaming, for the girl to respond.

But Astrid merely cast him a sideways glance. "He said all that, did he?"

Baldur chuffed again and plopped down in the snow. He turned to stare at Tosk, exasperation reflected in his dark eyes. Tosk refused to blush, although he did allow himself to bristle in indignation. "Well, it is what you meant, was it not?" he complained. "Bear speech is terribly difficult to translate. I gather you do not appreciate the difficulty of my position here."

"What exactly is your position?" Astrid asked, her lips turning down in a frown. He would never have described her as ugly, even with her hideous scars, but her intense scowl did nothing to improve her looks.

Something in her tone stoked his ire. She clearly did *not* appreciate his position. Any kind thoughts he had been harboring for her began to wither. "I have many duties," he replied, his tone as stiff as the indignant arch to his spine. "I'm sure you wouldn't understand."

"I am sure I would not," the girl agreed gravely.

Baldur chuffed his misery and turned to lumber back toward the fortress.

Curse them! This was not going at all like he had planned. Tosk flicked his tail against the gathering darkness as the dragon girl trudged after the bear, as the Watchers continued to watch and Kenna continued to sulk. He was annoyed because they were trying his patience, because he could do nothing to make them see reason, and because he knew as well as any of them that time would not grant them an amnesty forever. The dragon was coming. Of that, he had no doubt. The bone woman had reminded Kenna of that fact only a few days ago.

And although the bone woman was many things, she was rarely wrong.

The Watchers returned to their familiar haunts in the great ash tree. Hugin, the older brother, sat far above the prince's window while Munin sat nearly level with it, close to the trunk to avoid gusts of strong wind. He liked to be close to the window so he might hear what was being said within.

The young raven sighed and hunched his wings around his head. How he missed the warmth of the sun. In the far north, the summers were short and not nearly warm enough for his liking, but he thrived in the short sweetness of the those days.

These brutal winters wore on him like a lingering cough.

"Cru-u-uk," his brother said from above, in the raven tongue. Hugin was tired and wanted to retire for the night. Munin should agree with him. Nothing else would happen this night, not if Odin's son followed his usual patterns. He would settle the girl in her new chambers and leave her to her own devices for the remainder of the night. They would not meet again until morning.

There was nothing to see. He should retire gladly.

But he lingered.

Somewhere in the darkness, he knew another raven lurked in the darkness. She would be hiding, doing what ravens do best—watching from the shadows.

He understood her pain. Long ago, when she had been new in her service to the Raven King, Kenna had been forced to come face to face with the reality of her circumstances. Taking Odin's oath of servitude was not a matter to be taken lightly. Servants were as necessary as breath to their masters, but they would never be one with them.

Kenna had learned that the hard way, and Munin felt for her.

She had planned for a life as a bone girl, learning the secrets of the Mist and how to bend those secrets to the good of the land. Instead, she became neither bone girl nor Watcher, but something in between.

He rubbed his beak against his wing. The in between was never easy.

Hugin dropped down beside him, croaking deep in his throat. "Are you done ruminating?" he asked, pretending to be more annoyed than he truly was. Munin allowed an amused sound to reverberate from his chest. Naturally, Hugin would compare contemplation to the ruminations of a cow chewing his cud. Hugin had never been one to flatter.

"I am," Munin replied. His brother clucked in approval and trotted down the length of the branch and leapt into the evening air. Munin allowed himself one last moment to search for Kenna in the shadows, but she was hidden too well. He shook himself and moved to follow his brother.

There would always be time for more ruminations on the morrow. Time was something a Watcher had in abundance.

Baldur hunkered on his bed of pelts, his eyes hidden behind his paw. Nearby, Kenna hissed at him in frustration. Tosk was curled in a ball on top of Baldur's back, yawning in between his sleepy interpretations.

"She says this girl is different," Tosk said, and he yawned before continuing. "She said that you should sweep the dragon girl off her feet and fall madly in love with—"

Kenna squawked loudly, the sound short and shrill.

"That was rude," the squirrel argued. "I do not *extrapolate*. You probably do not even know what that word means."

Kenna bobbed her head toward him and warbled a heated, lengthy speech that Baldur assumed must involve her definitions of "extrapolation."

"Apparently you *do* know what it means," Tosk grumbled. "Very well. She says you must stop feeling sorry for yourself and take action."

"I do not feel sorry for myself," Baldur complained. He had reached that place beyond exhaustion where even the prospect of sleep did nothing to ease his weariness. "I am merely tired, and you two plague me when I am tired. Can we not resume this conversation in the morning? After I have had a chance to properly examine the girl?"

Tosk rose, turned in a circle, and resituated himself into another ball. "I do not want to tell her that. I would rather not get pecked, if it please you, Odin-son."

Baldur huffed and stuffed his other paw into his mouth. He did not have to look to know that they were both receiving the evil eye from their companion. "Please," he mumbled around the pads of his foot. "I just wish to sleep. I will try harder tomorrow. I swear it."

Kenna said something in a softer tone, her warble boarding on melancholy.

"She wishes to know what you thought of the dragon girl," Tosk murmured and yawned again.

Baldur stifled a sigh. He wished he did have something to tell her, so that their indecipherable exchange might at least be a pleasant one, but he had little hopes for the dragon slayer's daughter. Yes, she was fair enough, outside the scarring, but she did not seem open. She carried herself like a wild animal who had been caught in a snare and escaped, and who now determined she would never be caught again.

She had walls built around her higher than the wall of Jar Rann.

He removed his damp paw from his mouth. "She seems to be a strong girl," he conceded, in a growl that sounded as melancholy as Kenna's warble. "I cannot say more without spending time with her. Only time will tell. Only time."

Tosk did not seem eager to translate. Baldur waited a moment, wondering if he was considering how to reword Baldur's little speech with a positive spin, but after a long moment it became apparent the rascal had fallen asleep.

He heard the sound of wings, of short claws scrabbling over the windowsill. When he looked a few moments later, Kenna was gone. The darkness outside the window felt endless somehow, as if it were a void that had swallowed up the bird, a void that threatened to swallow him as well.

"I *am* trying," he whispered to himself, even though he knew no one was listening. Kenna was long gone and Tosk had lost himself to the realm of dreams. The little fellow inhaled a wheezy breath that rapidly escalated into a nasal snore. "I *am* trying," he repeated. "But I fear this girl will be just like all the others. There is simply nothing there."

There never was. It seemed that whatever spark gave him the capacity to love had been snuffed out long ago. He was so tired of hoping for something that he knew in his heart would never happen. Even Kenna no longer loved him. How could he expect any other woman to care for him?

Baldur fell asleep remembering the sounds of an early spring storm, but when he dreamed, he dreamed of fire rising from the mountains in the form of dragon's breath.

FIVE

It had been three days, and Astrid feared she would surely be sent home in disgrace.

It had not occurred to her until after she left Sandfell and journeyed alone to the fortress in the hills how much she risked with this venture. When she failed—*if* she failed—she would lose the respect of all.

She had volunteered to take the place of a slave only to risk becoming one. Astrid slid her hand into her pocket to finger the dragon rune. She simply did not have it in her to play the happy house servant, making meals and cleaning and keeping the fires burning.

Odin's son would not even allow her to hunt for their food. According to Tosk, this was one task Baldur insisted on performing himself. It was the one task she would have enjoyed doing. The bear was gracious enough to allow her to prepare his kills when he brought them home, but there was no pleasure in cleaning a carcass caught by another.

Snow dusted the hood and shoulders of her long coat. The doe hide was fur-lined and tickled her ears, but she preferred that to the bitter northern wind ripping across the Niflheim. Jar Rann sat on a rocky plateau unprotected by the forested lowlands, so there was nothing to deflect Skadi's wrathful winds.

Nor was there anything to protect her from the unnatural elements at work within the ringed fortress. She had never known the companionship of many friends, yet this isolation disturbed her in ways her lonely childhood had not.

Jar Rann had once been a hub of activity where traders and hunters and travelers alike came to barter and swap tales. Astrid remembered coming here when she was but a little girl. It had awed her then, with its sights and smells and thronging crowds—with the burly men smashing their fists against their shields as they told tales both loud and interesting, the sort of tales that caused her mother to wrap her cold hands over Astrid's eager ears. Astrid had always loved the tales of the dragons, the stories of the warriors risking their life's blood to battle the monstrous creatures that plagued the helpless. She was not so interested in their outspoken wives, who like her mother gathered around the traders' carts, haggling over beads and furs and treats for their squealing children.

Nothing of those days remained. Now the fortress was abandoned, still as a tomb, empty as a barren woman. There were no traders, no haggling women and no children racing through the crowds. The only visitors who entered Jar Rann were the thralls sent to satisfy the Trials, and even they did not stay long. The day the curse took Baldur, everything changed.

It was as if life had stopped for Jar Rann—not time, because that continued to spiral away from them. The buildings fell into disrepair, the once-traveled paths were buried in snow drifts, and even the air felt stale and heavy as if it grew stagnant from disuse.

For the first time in her life she actually longed for human conversation. Baldur and the raven had been cursed into silence, and Tosk might as well have been included in that silence, for all the pleasure his talk gave her.

Something stirred behind her. She turned to see the little devil hopping in and out of her footprints trying to catch up with her. He had been following her all morning but had finally found something to distract himself a short while ago. And now he was back, grinning at her as he approached. She sighed. The only thing of life in the fortress seemed to be the Gossip—Tosk did not seem to care that Jar Rann no longer lived up to its fabled glory. She almost envied his blind optimism.

Nothing seemed to dampen his spirit.

"Kenna had muskrat for breakfast—she found it down by the river, frozen in the ice," Tosk announced, as if this were news that should interest her. "What else? Oh, I heard them speaking about you last night. Again. Baldur thinks you can't boil water, you know." The little beast spoke cheerfully, as if this report should be good tidings to her. Without taking a breath, he launched into another speech.

Her heart felt heavy. It was true she lacked finesse around a dinner fire. She had not been prepared for her Trial the way most maidens were. Her preparations had been of a darker sort.

When she still ignored him, the red squirrel ran up the back of her leg, snagging hold of her coat and worming his way up the inside of it until he perched inside her hood beside her ear. The long tufts on his ears tickled her cheek.

He smelled musty like parchments and damp like wet dog. "Are you listening?"

She was not. Astrid moved to finger the bone again. She paused to stamp her feet and glance across the courtyard, through the naked branches of the ash tree at the center, the squirrel's tinny voice in her ear. The smooth bit of bone felt soothing between her fingers, a piece of herself in this strange place. She could see the bear, holed up in his tower, squinting at them through the fog of heavy snowflakes. Unease churned in her belly like a tangle of snakes. She reached up to cover her scars, as if they could somehow reveal the secrets she kept.

Did he suspect why she had come?

Tosk squeezed her ear lobe with his tiny paws. "Dragon girl! I said, have you figured out where he's hiding the treasure yet?" Still holding onto her ear, he shuddered, apparently with uncontrollable delight.

"Oh, do hush," Astrid complained and flicked him on the stomach. "Enough of your gossip." She'd heard all the stories in Sandfell about the past wealth of Jar Rann buried in the snow somewhere, but she believed naught of it.

If Baldur had a fortune at his disposal, he could afford to buy himself a wife.

They would have no need for the Trials.

She deliberately set her feet to the narrow path once again. She should return to the longhouse. Her body temperature was high from exertion, but her cheeks prickled and felt stiff and chapped from exposure. Still, she lingered. It was a small show of rebellion, probably obvious to none but herself. Her father would have recognized her stubbornness as disobedience, but he was not here.

"May your boots chafe," Astrid muttered the half-hearted curse and instantly repented of it. Sigurd was probably too drunk to know if his boots chafed him. Besides, she knew all too well the power of curses.

It was after all the reason she had come here. Rather, it was one of the reasons.

She heard the screeching of unoiled hinges and a loud bellow. The squirrel yelped and clung to her tangle of braids. She tried to dislodge him by wiggling her shoulder, but he rebounded and flipped his tail in her face. From the longhouse doorway, the bear roared at her. Astrid waited. Tosk cocked his good ear toward the kitchen. Baldur bellowed again, his breath fogging on the wind in irritated bursts, and he angrily thrust his front paws off the ground only to come thudding back down. Emphatically.

She was being summoned.

Tosk scrabbled across the courtyard, bounding in and out of snowdrifts, and right up Baldur's front leg and shoulder. Most likely, he was concocting some vile tale of her. He had a gift for that sort of thing. Astrid pursed her lips but turned to obey. She left the path she had carved with her own footsteps and trudged toward the longhouse, through knee high snow drifts. It slowed her down, which bothered her naught a bit.

It bothered the bear a great deal. He lumbered outdoors, his ungainly body draped with a patchwork cloak of deer hides large enough to clothe four grown men. He looked ridiculous, as usual, but this was a thought Astrid intended to take to her grave rather than share.

After all, it was hardly the sort of thing potential lovers said to one another.

She passed by him without comment and did not flinch when the door slammed behind her. She heard a heavy plop as snow slid from the roof to the frozen ground. Tosk chittered and raced about the expansive room, making little sense but a great deal of general mischief. Baldur growled and swept a paw, but the squirrel dodged it and continued his revelry.

Baldur grabbed her sleeve between his teeth and tugged her toward the hearth, where a black pot smoked over an untended fire. He fumbled at the lid with his claws and chuffed at her, indicating the scorched remains of what should have been their evening stew.

This must be the only bear in the Niflheim who refused to eat raw meat.

"I apologize," she said, feeling her failure down to the core of her bones. She had forgotten all about the stew...again.

He snarled something that indicated her apology was not accepted, while Tosk rolled with laughter on the floor. "Oh, my giddy aunt! He just said you—"

"You do not need to repeat whatever it was he said," Astrid interrupted, her voice sharp. Trying to suppress a rising sense of despair, she ripped one mitten off at a time and set them down on the plank table. Baldur waited as she peeled the scarf from around her neck and removed first her overcoat, and then several layers beneath that. She tugged off her boots and set them neatly beside the smoking remains of dinner. Astrid then turned to reach for her outer garments, to put them away.

This was too much for Baldur. He bellowed and swatted the pot against the stone hearth wall. This time, when the contents of the pot spilled across her feet, she did flinch. But Baldur did not move to throttle her—as her father would have surely done—but turned and lumbered from the room, knocking over everything he could find between there and his tower high above her.

Tosk whimpered and slunk to his cubby high in the corner, properly chastised.

Astrid sighed. She did not like feeling chastised, especially when serving dinner was at the absolute bottom of her priorities. She was going to disappoint everyone. That's all there was to it: she could not please them all. It was not easy living a lie, not even here in Jar Rann where nothing was what it seemed.

Some girls were not destined to fall in love, no matter how desperately they may wish to.

SIX

The long days had turned into long weeks. Kenna sulked in the highest branches of the ash tree. The sky arched above her, gray and bland, the sun masked behind low-lying clouds. The bleakness of the day did nothing to improve her mood.

Baldur was not ready to send the girl home even though no progress had been made in the three weeks she had been there. Kenna did not understand what he was waiting for.

A breeze hit her, and she ruffled her feathers, agitated. This was not at all how she had hoped things would turn out. She had hoped this girl would be different—and she was different, but in the wrong sort of way.

Granted, Astrid actually wanted to be here. It was plain as day, although Kenna could not imagine the girl's true intentions.

The dragon slayer's daughter was not like the usual selections: most of the chosen maids were prepared for their Trial. They could sing, clean and sew. Some could even recite the ancient lays. Even though they were terrified and unwilling participants, they could all behave.

They could all cook.

Kenna paced along the tree branch, hissing to herself and wondering why this girl had come to them when she was so obviously ill-prepared.

She would never break the curse.

Something deep inside the raven stirred, and it was not pleasant. It was dark and painful and plagued her excessively.

It was guilt.

An outburst interrupted her black musing. She tried ignoring him, but the squirrel raced up the tree, only growing more insistent. As Tosk scrabbled toward her on all fours, the slender branch bucked beneath their combined weight. Kenna hissed at him and clung tighter. He stopped beside her, yanking at the tufts on his ears as he shouted at her.

"What is it? I can't understand you!" she squawked and swatted him with a wing. Tosk did a frustrated little dance and tugged his ears down around his chin. He clutched them there, his small body quivering. Kenna felt a thrill of alarm. The squirrel was clearly agitated beyond words.

Unlike the rest of them, Tosk was never at a loss for words.

"They've gone mad!" he finally shouted, his paws pounding together, still full of ear tufts. "I think they're going to kill each other!"

Kenna croaked in disbelief and thrust off the branch, leaving Tosk to howl and cling to the lurching branch. She expected no better from that worthless dragon girl, but it took a great deal to push Baldur to violence. She landed on a high window sill to the longhouse and wedged through the shutters propped ajar by the snow. She could hear the girl shouting as she fluttered onto the rafters.

"I am sick to death of the sulking—and the cooking and the—the chores! I hate chores! I am not here to be your slave—"

Baldur roared something back at her so loudly the very rafters seemed to quake in fear. Kenna leaned forward to see what was happening below her. Astrid stood on one side of the fire pit, brandishing a broom like a weapon, while Baldur stood back on his hind paws, towering over her. He swiped a paw at the air and roared again.

"That's another thing!" Astrid shouted and stabbed toward him with the bristly end of her broom, as if he were a wee mouse and not teeth and claws and four times her size. "I am wearied to the bone with the roaring! Where is Tosk? For once, can we not have a respectable conversation? I did not come here to coddle a child—your tantrums are beneath you. Beneath me!"

Baldur smacked away her broom with a stunned bellow, his claws shredding the bristles and scattering them into the smoldering fire. Astrid darted back and jabbed him with the other end of the stick, hard enough he chuffed in response and dropped to his forepaws.

"No wonder you cannot find a wife! We cannot understand anything when you growl like a cub that's lost its mam! Will you not tell me what you want? Just speak with me! Please!"

It felt as if time skidded to a wrenching halt. Kenna's heart beat so violently she feared it would break free of her chest and drop to the ground far below. Baldur groaned and swiped a paw at his mouth, as if he had eaten something terrible and wanted to hack it back out. He dropped his nose to the ground, grunting and growling in turn. His mouth worked soundlessly, and then he *spoke*.

"I can speak with you," Baldur said, the words as rusty as an abandoned door hinge. "Thank you for asking."

That voice! Kenna thought and closed her eyes. She could already remember the last time she had heard him speak. It had been such a long time ago. They had both said things that night, terrible things, the sort of things that curses were made of.

It was the night she lost control and ruined everything.

How had the girl known to ask him? Had it merely been a blunder? Careless words said in a fit of her temper? Had Tosk broken his promise and given her a hint? She would not put it past him. Even the gravest of oaths could not temper that squirrel's tattling tongue.

Baldur growled and took a step toward the girl. "You had to ask me to speak with you," he said, his maw forming each word with awkward precision. He rose to tower over the dragon slayer's daughter. "It's one of the rules of the Trials—to test your sincerity, perhaps your cleverness. No one has ever asked."

Astrid stared at him, mouth open. She gulped abruptly and jabbed the stick at him. "I cannot believe that you can *speak,* after all these years of bellowing at your visitors as if they were simpletons!" As she spoke, her words grew louder and louder, her color deepening with anger.

"I had no choice!" he bellowed back. "I wish I could change things, but I cannot. I am as bound by these ridiculous Trials as the girls." This last phrase came out in almost a whisper.

When Astrid lowered her broom handle and cocked her head to one side as she studied him, Kenna felt a pang twist her insides. Silence filled the longhouse once again. She could not breathe, her black eyes wide and unblinking. This was what she had wanted all along; this was what she feared more than anything in the world.

"The Trials are not your doing?" Astrid asked, as if this question were somehow more important than any other.

Baldur snorted and sat down hard, turning his face from her. "I would never have chosen this," he sighed. "The Trials were my mother's doing. If you believe nothing else, dragon girl, believe this."

Kenna scuttled back toward the window. The dark place inside her was growing more painful. This was quickly becoming an exchange she no longer wished to be a part of.

The squirrel was there, appearing from nowhere as he was wont to do. "I told you," he said, doing another of his irritating little dances. "She's the one."

Kenna's chest grew even tighter, the dark space pressing against every part of her until there was almost nothing of her left. Tosk was the last creature she wanted to see right now. She tried to peck him, but he dodged and disappeared into one of his secret hideaways.

Kenna blinked and nuts began rolling out of the hole. Tosk tumbled after, wailing, and tried to pounce on his escaping stores, only to have them vanish beneath his touch.

It was, after all, only a trick.

It seemed she was not good for much else. Kenna squeezed through the narrow gap on the window, back into the cold. Upset, Tosk barreled after her. "It could never have been you," he shouted, touching the place from which her anger truly stemmed.

"Be gone with you!" Kenna shrieked. Her wings beat furiously, lifting her away from that accursed, ear-tufted gossip and toward the south tower. But she changed her mind when she caught sight of the two dark splotches hulking against the snow on the tower roof. She veered east, fluttering down to the store room roof. She craned her neck backwards.

The ravens were there, watching.

Kenna's blood ran cold. She fluffed her feathers and huddled deep into herself, hissing as she gazed up at the two shadows on the tower roof, at the Raven King's spies.

Tosk scrambled down beside her. "They're watching you, bird." For once he did not sound as if he were laughing at her. Kenna shivered.

Hugin gazed down on her with one dark, glittering eye, and Munin perched beside him, gently bobbing back and forth. Munin's beak parted as if he wished to speak, but he made no noise. He merely looked at her.

How many times had she seen them over the past fortnight? When she began to figure the number of days, she realized that they had been present more often than not.

This alarming frequency could only be an omen.

It meant something was about to happen, something worth watching, and whatever it was, good or bad, Kenna knew it would be the ruin of her. Frigg's prophecy had finally caught up with them. Perhaps there was still time to save Baldur, but it would mean the end of her.

Frigg had foreseen that, too.

As the dark space engulfed her, Kenna took to the skies, to the one place Tosk could not follow. Her keening cries were lost on the bitter wind. No one heard, no one but the Watchers, and they did not care about her. They were here for Baldur, because the end was drawing near. The signs all pointed to the times: the dying rose bush, the dragon slayer's daughter, the shifting in the curse. It all pointed to Frigg's foreseen nightmare. Time had finally caught up with them.

The dragon was coming.

SEVEN

The next morning, Baldur found Astrid in the center of the longhouse, head pillowed on a crudely bound book she had been reading. The fire had given way to gray-dusted embers. He wanted to be angry with her for staying up all night, because it meant she would want to sleep the day away, but he tempered his impatience. Instead, he picked up a log with his teeth and nosed it into the embers, stirring it about until the log sparked and began to glow at the edges.

He turned to the dragon slayer's daughter and nudged her hand. She woke at once, her other hand moving to rub the one he had touched with his cold nose. She laughed faintly and closed the book. "Is it late?" she asked.

Baldur growled a negative before he remembered. After all this time suffering in isolation, it no longer felt natural to speak. "No," he said aloud. "You've slept the night and half the day."

Astrid sat up and rubbed her arms. "It's cold."

"It is." He nudged the pelt she sat on with his paw, and she moved to burrow beneath it. He dropped down beside her, so that she was cocooned between him and the fire. Their exchange felt awkward and strained, even though they had ceased arguing not long after he began speaking. It seemed Astrid did truly respond well to calm conversation. It was not as if she had forgiven him for all the confusion and tempers, but she seemed to have accepted them.

She sighed, a contented sound, and seemed to go back to sleep. "Are you in good humor today?" she asked.

He thought for a moment, wondering if her question was serious or jest. "I am always in good humor," he quipped. "For a bear."

She snorted and propped herself up by the elbows. "I wish to ask you a question." It did not seem like a request, so he did not bother giving his consent. Astrid seemed the sort who did as she pleased. She was not shy, this one. He waited, somewhat uncomfortably, wondering what sort of awkward question would necessitate an announcement.

"Frigg's prophecy," she said. "How do you foresee it ending?"

Baldur closed his eyes and turned his face away. This was not a topic he wished to discuss. It preoccupied his every waking thought and haunted each sleeping one.

"Baldur?" Her voice sounded small, and he felt sorry for the pressure he must have put on her, bringing her here under such high expectations. They had no choice, however. The rules of the Trials were laid out for the both of them. It must not sit well with her that many had gone before her and failed—many who were so better prepared.

"I wish to ask *you* a question." Baldur turned his face toward her, his head resting on one of his dastardly cumbersome paws.

Astrid made a face. "You have not answered mine yet," she protested.

"This is my house, not yours. Why were you sent here? It was my understanding the lot only fell on the thralls."

Astrid's expression soured even further. "I do not wish to answer *that* question," she said.

"This is my house."

"And, as you so plainly stated, I am not a thrall and feel no obligation to answer your question if you do not answer mine," she hedged.

So that was it, then. She did have a secret. Baldur huffed and closed his eyes again. The confirmation should not disturb him unduly— most everyone did have a secret—but for some reason, Astrid's secret seemed the sort that might backfire and bite one in the hind quarters.

This was not going well.

She had asked him how he thought his mother's prophecy would end—if it would end in fire as Frigg predicted—or if his fate might be averted. Frigg had predicted that he might be spared if he fell in love, and if the girl returned his affection. That was the catch. The bond had to be strong, both directions.

That's why Frigg had initiated the Trials, to find him a suitable partner. It would not have been so difficult a task had Kenna not been a factor. The old familiar ache returned to him as he remembered and regretted. It was his own foolishness that brought this on him, that had turned him into this animal and Kenna into a bird. He did not blame her. She had suffered as much for her mistake as he had for his.

And for that very reason, Baldur already knew how this would end.

"I think I will die," he said, staring into the darkness behind his eyelids. He imagined fire, crackling and blue with dragon heat. Was this everything he had become? He was nothing outside the dragon. It consumed everything. Somewhere along the way he had lost himself. It was as if knowing his future had robbed him of any sort of present—of any sort of *being*. He existed. Nothing more. "I think I will fight the dragon and die."

Astrid was still. "It might not happen that way," she suggested, her voice naught but a whisper. "The bones did not choose me. I offered myself."

A willing Trial. This he already knew. Hearing it from her own mouth made the fact more poignant. He contemplated at great length, but he could not decide whether it was a good or worrisome thing. He had learned long ago to not place his hopes idly. Even his own father had given up such hopes. Odin busied himself with the giants of the north rather than with Baldur's dilemma.

This pained him, too. Even his own father had given up on him.

Baldur rose and shook himself briskly. He paused to look down at the dragon slayer's daughter. He hoped she could see the humanity in his eyes, even if the rest of him screamed animal. "You say the choice was yours. That this might not happen the way I think it will. So I ask you: do you love me? Astrid? Do you feel anything for me, dragon girl?"

Astrid did not answer. She ducked her head, so that her fair hair fell over her face and concealed it. Baldur's hopes could not truly be dashed, because he had not allowed himself to hope in the first place.

"Then I will die a hero's death," he said, not unkindly. "Think well of me, when the Valkyrie come, and tell your children how you knew me, and how I died with honor."

He did not blame her for not knowing her own heart. How could he, when he did not even know his own?

EIGHT

The bear was not making this easy.

The sword split the air with a hiss and struck the bale of straw which quickly transformed into a battered heap. Astrid spun and struck again, and again, turning her ire into motion. She had seen the look on Baldur's face when she confessed.

I offered myself, she had told him, like an idiot, as if she had real intentions of falling in love with him and saving him from this curse. It did not escape her notice, the quick flash of life in the bear's somber gaze. Nor was it lost on her how quickly that hope disappeared.

"Stupid girl!" she hissed as she swung away from the annihilated bale. She snatched up a round wooden shield from the store room floor without breaking her motion. She swung back to the front and drove into the straw, battering and jabbing in turn. When the straw failed to prove a worthy combatant, she hammered the walls, split open bags of seed grain, and chopped a wooden bucket to splinters. She did not quit until she lay panting on the ground with the remains of her opponents strewn around her. She blew some straw off her face and shouted, striking the ground with her elbow, repeatedly, until her entire arm throbbed.

A squawk from the rafters informed her she was not alone. She opened her eyes and saw the raven glaring down at her, head turned so that it looked through one, hateful eye. Astrid grabbed a fistful of grain and flung it toward the ceiling. It only came pelting back down on her. "I did not ask you! Go away!"

The raven dove for her, and Astrid rolled clear, but not before that sharp beak pecked her on the back of the head. She wrapped her arms around her head and waited until the flapping of wings faded into silence. She moaned, rubbed the sore spot on her skull and crooked one arm over her head, smothering the scars on her cheek.

As the tears welled behind her eyes, Astrid hated herself for this weakness. Father would be appalled by her foolish display, as he was appalled by about everything she did. Had she been a son perhaps she would have managed to please him. Had she been the daughter of his first love perhaps he would not have hated her at every turn. Had she been a thousand things other than what she was perhaps he would have loved her.

As it was, she was but a girl, the unwanted result of an unwanted union. She had but one purpose and one purpose only. She could not let herself be distracted from it. If she did this one final thing—this final, terrible thing—perhaps he would finally see her as the loyal daughter she was.

Maybe he would finally love her as she loved him.

Astrid's emotions cooled as her body temperature dropped, soothed by the drafts sneaking through the crude walls around her. She picked herself up, gathered her weapons, and abandoned the vandalized store room. The sun set in the western sky, ablaze in scarlet and orange light that reflected off ice and snow. Astrid paused, her breath a fog around her face. It should have been a beautiful sight, and it would have been for a normal person. But for a dragon slayer, a red sky only meant one thing.

It meant—somewhere—a dragon was awake.

The red smear lay to the south, away from Sandfell, so she felt no concern for her mother and the other villagers. She told herself she should feel concern for someone. Wherever the dragon was, be it great or small, it was sure to cause trouble. Yet, Astrid had to admit to herself the only emotion she felt was relief. A dragon was awake.

It meant her quest was not futile, because the dragon had always been her quest. She hoped to find the dragon that had long plagued her father, and by finding it she would finally gain her father's love and respect. She had been distracted by the bear because he had become something other than what she'd imagined. He was not all beast. There was a sadness to him, perhaps even a kindness. His fits of temper seemed to be driven by pain and desperation, not cruelty.

Yet this knowledge did not change why she was here.

Surely, Baldur would not expect her to give up everything for him, for his Trials. Perhaps there was enough sadness and kindness in him that he would allow her to embrace her own destiny—that he would let her walk her own path, rather than be bound by his.

After all, how could he expect differently? She was a dragon slayer's daughter.

Of course she would be here for the dragon.

NINE

When Kenna did not go to him, Baldur came to find her. She had expected no less.

Therefore she had done her best to find a hole in the darkness deep enough to swallow her, so that she would not be found unless she wished it. Baldur was not the only creature in this fortress she wished to avoid. But Baldur's instincts were as remarkable as ever. He found her on the south wall where she hunkered beneath the shelter of a pine bough hanging over the wooden palisade, its branches laden with snow.

Baldur sat down and cocked his head to one side, nose sniffing the midnight air.

"I waited up for you," he said.

She stirred and eked an annoyed sound, for his benefit.

"I waited up," he repeated. "As did Tosk, who is now snoring on my hearth. Did you not wish an update this evening? Considering."

She cawed in response, although she knew he would not understand her answer.

He shook himself, as if annoyed. "I wish to speak with you. It has been some time since we spoke together."

And it would be some time hence before they did. It was difficult to hold a conversation with only one party. She tucked her beak beneath a wing and hoped he would go away. Instead of complying, he huffed. "Come down, Kenna. That is not a request."

She wanted to disobey, but he was a son of Odin and she had vowed to serve him until her death. It was the duty of the raven-kind to serve the Raven King. Kenna slipped from the wall and dropped down to Baldur, landing on his back. She scrambled up to sit on his shoulder, feathers fluffed in agitation.

"Thank you."

She hissed at him, but it was half-hearted at best and petulant at worst. He turned about and began to lumber back toward the longhouse. Kenna rocked up and down with each step. "There is a matter of great importance I wish to discuss with you." His voice was slightly muffled, his nose to the ground as if he watched where his paws landed in the heavy snow. "I think we both know what I must say."

Kenna felt the last bit of herself shrivel. She did know of what he must speak, but when he said it, the last remnant of the girl she had been would disappear. Only the terrible bird would remain. She had always hoped this day would come, but now that it had, she wished she could unravel time and go back to the beginning. It had been hard, but not as hard as this.

They reached the longhouse, but Baldur sat down in the snow instead of entering. Kenna could hear Tosk's breathy snores from within. She wished she could stop her ears, but Baldur had not yet said his piece. He must tell her that he finally found a woman to love and be loved by.

He had come to tell her that girl was Astrid.

In the space of a few hours, everything had changed.

"When the time comes," Baldur said at last, his voice part growl, part man sound. "When the time comes, Kenna, you are to stay away from the dragon."

She snapped her head toward him, her beak a mere space from his ear. She croaked, the sound unpleasant even to her.

"That is not a request."

She rocked back and forth, battling between obedience to him and adherence to her vow. If in disobedience she might save his life, was it acceptable to disobey?

"I would have your word, Kenna. It is the last thing I will ever ask of you," Baldur murmured. "So I am asking: will you speak with me? Tonight? Will you give me your word?"

She felt a thrill like liquid fire course through her body. It began at her wing tips and worked backward until it spun around her vocal chords. At first it squeezed, as if choking her, but then her throat filled with air, and her lungs expanded.

She felt the words on her tongue—old, familiar words she had thought she would never speak again. All this time they had been bound in silence, unable to speak to one another even when they wished it. After all, one could not ask when one could not speak. Kenna was sure Frigg had done this deliberately, because she blamed Kenna for Baldur's plight.

By freeing Baldur, Astrid had given Kenna the chance to speak again as well.

He had asked her.

"Baldur," she croaked. He shuddered, most likely from cold. "You should not have asked."

"I had to."

She nipped at his ear. "There isn't time for this. There is only time for *her.*"

"I fear there is not time even for that," he rumbled. "You must give me your word. I insist. Your word that you will stay out of this."

Kenna hissed and clawed around to his other shoulder. "I will not! You cannot give up, not now. Not when we are so close. I will give you my word only if you give yours—that you will not give up. You will keep trying until the very end. That is my price."

He sighed. "Must everything come with a price?" He meant it to sound clever, she knew, but it only sounded sad.

"Yes," she hissed. "It must."

"Then I give my word."

"And I give mine." She lifted from his shoulder and flapped up to the lower branches of the ash tree. Baldur ambled into the longhouse. He paused to look back, but when she said nothing further, he lowered his nose to the ground and entered.

Kenna heard wings above her, high in the branches. She hunched into herself. Apparently, Baldur was not the only one who had found her this night. She heard hissing from above, one deep and insistent, the other breathy and persuasive.

She did not know who won the argument, but finally one of Odin's birds dropped down beside her on the branch. She tucked her beak to her chest and twisted away, unwilling to even look at him.

"Good Eve," the raven said, his voice surprisingly mild. "My brother is of the persuasion that Odin's son has fallen beyond help. That the Trials are nearly over."

She squinted at him through one eye. The Watchers had never spoken to her before. Never. Kenna lifted her head, beak parted. Munin's feathers rustled as he moved closer to her, so that they sat side by side in the darkness. "But my brother thinks too much, I fear," he confessed.

"And you?" Kenna asked, in raven tongue, because it had become as natural as thought to her. "What do you think?"

Munin answered in kind. "My brother says I do not think at all. That I only feel."

"What do you feel then?"

He turned toward her, gazing at her through his left eye first and then twisting his head to see through the right. She felt a shiver work its way throughout the whole of her bird body. "I feel there is always hope," he said, "until there is none. And then there is sacrifice, so that hope may return."

It was as if he had cut her to the heart, his beak rammed into her chest, ripping her open. The pain leaked from her like life blood. Kenna keened and rocked back and forth. It always came back to this.

It always came back to the end.

One of them had to die.

TEN

"What is that?" Astrid asked when Baldur entered the longhouse, a potted bowl of dirt sticking from his mouth. They had not spoken since their unfortunate encounter the day before. Baldur mumbled something as he eased the lopsided piece of pottery onto the ground, where she sat pouring over a crude map. She casually draped her arm over the map, concealing it. "I beg pardon?"

Baldur sneezed. His mouth worked awkwardly, probably full of dirt, and he spat to one side. "It's a rose bush," he croaked. "It is mine."

"Oh." Astrid tried to ease the old parchment closer to her body, without drawing attention to herself. His timing could not have been less timely. "Why is it in here?"

"It needs tending."

She eyed the bush with no small amount of skepticism. The plant sported little besides spindly arms and jagged thorns. It had but one rose, withering on the end of a bent stem. She knew nothing of gardening, but after yesterday she had no desire to admit that.

"I was hoping you would revive it."

"*Revive it?*" she echoed, her eyebrows arching toward her hairline. "Baldur, forgive me, but that bush looks beyond help." When his expression fell, she hastily cleared her throat. "I am hardly an expert on *reviving*."

"No, I suppose you are not," he said, his attention on his paws. He stuffed one of them into his mouth and chewed on it. There was something alarmingly endearing about the act, and she quickly tore her gaze away.

A familiar scampering noise announced the squirrel's arrival. He emerged from a pile of coon and fox pelts in the corner, his mouth open in a yawn. He scratched at his side and glared at them. When they both ignored him, Tosk curled into a ball, tucking his head beneath his tail.

"Might you at least try something?" Baldur mumbled around his paw. Astrid watched the squirrel, not him, and noted each telling twitch of Tosk's tail. He was eavesdropping, naturally.

"Is it so important?" she sighed, annoyed with the squirrel, annoyed with Baldur.

He removed the paw from his mouth. It hung in midair, damp from his gnawing. "I would not have asked if it wasn't." He was beginning to sound bothered. "Try giving it some fertilizer, perhaps, or—"

"Fertilizer!" Astrid echoed, louder than she intended. She blushed and shook her head. "Honestly, Baldur, I have seen your store rooms. You are sorely lacking in horses and chickens. Where on earth shall I find fertilizer?"

He growled and thumped his paw to the ground. "I do not care where you find it. Ask Tosk, for all I care. With the amount of my stores he consumes, he ought to be good for that much."

Astrid choked on her disbelief, and Tosk sat bolt upright, clearly outraged. He scrambled over to sit on the hearth beside Astrid, his paws shaking at the sky as he expounded on his indignation. Their response seemed to push Baldur to the edge of his patience. "I am not asking," he bellowed, rising up on his back legs so that he towered over them. "You said you chose yourself, girl. Then do your part. Enough of your laziness and book reading. This can never work if you do not *try,* and I have made a promise that I will not stop trying until—"

She could take no more. "Why I came is my own business, and has nothing to do with you!" Astrid exclaimed, outraged that he thought her lazy. Her cheeks flamed with temper, and she warned herself to be still.

"Then why did you come?" he growled. "What are you trying to find in all my archives that you cannot find out from me? There is no treasure, girl. There never was." He dropped to all fours, scattering logs and woven baskets of kindling as he lumbered toward her. Tosk yelped and dove for cover while Astrid scrambled backwards, crab-like, one fist trying to yank the parchment out of Baldur's sight. But his eyes were keen and he snagged it with a paw, rending it in two pieces. He glanced at the paper before ripping it to shreds with one swift movement. His dark eyes lifted to hers, and when he spoke again he spoke not with the force of a prince but with the deadly calm of a predator. "Why are you interested in the Caves?" He barely breathed the words.

Astrid dared not move. Baldur leaned over her, his nostrils flared, chest heaving. Once he understood why she had come, he would kick her out before she had a chance to see things through to the end.

"You have come to bait the dragon," he said, tonelessly. "Why else?" He inched backward, shaking his head side to side. Something inside her tore and began to ache. "What better way to lure a dragon than with treasure."

"Please, it is not what you think," she pleaded.

He roared at her, backed away—then roared again. "Do not make excuses! Do not tell me *stories!* I get enough of that from Tosk." The squirrel squeaked but dove back into the kindling basket. Baldur turned around and lumbered away.

"Baldur! Please—"

He spun back toward her with surprising swiftness. "You are not to go near the Caves. Do you understand me, girl? That is not a request." He pinned her with a hard stare. *"Do not go to the Caves."*

There was something almost frantic in him just then, but she did not have the heart to lie to him, to placate him. The truth was bitter, but perhaps it was better than the façade.

"I am sorry if my intentions frighten you," she began, hating how her voice shook. "I may not be here to *wed* you, but I am here to *help*—"

When Baldur swiped an angry paw against the ground, she broke off. "I will not have you lose your life for me! I do not want anyone to be hurt because of me."

"It's a little late for late," she breathed, the heat building in her face, her pulse thundering beneath her skin like a caged bird. Was he so naïve or did he simply not care about the girls he had sent back to Sandfell? Had he not once thought of them? Why should he suddenly be so concerned about the well-being of one girl when he had injured hundreds?

The fight seemed to drain out of him. He stared at her, as if she were a specter. "What do you mean?" he asked.

She clenched her jaw and wondered if she should even bother guarding her words. "Have you not once thought of the girls you've terrorized all these years?" she spat.

His nose lowered but he continued to stare at her, as if she were babbling in a foreign language. As if he had no idea what she was referring to. Was it possible he had no idea of the repercussions of his mother's Trials?

She opened her mouth to press him, but Baldur backed away from her, horror twisting his terrible face. He turned and barreled through the doorway, ripping the wooden door off its hinges.

Tosk dashed to her side. "Stupid girl! Stupid, stupid!" he shouted. When she ignored him, still too stunned to move, he bit her hand savagely. "Why would you tell him that?"

"Ouch! Ratatosk! I did not know it was a *secret,* rodent!"

"Rodent?" He spit at her. "Stupid girl! He desperately loves you!" The squirrel hopped all over and tugged at his ear tufts. When Astrid shot him a look, he paused with mouth gaping on whatever words he had planned next for her. "Fine," he conceded, "he desperately *wants* to love you. It is the same thing. Why will you not *behave?* Can't you do anything right? Stupid, stupid, stupid—"

"That's enough!" Astrid moved a foot toward him, and he bolted for the open doorway, still shouting at her. His words continued to echo in her mind even after he disappeared and his rants became unintelligible, and then silent. *Stupid, stupid, stupid.*

Had Baldur truly not known about the thralls?

ELEVEN

Kenna arrived in time to see Baldur charging across the yard, away from the longhouse. He made a sound that resembled a wounded animal caught in a hunter's snare. He tumbled through snow drifts, over stone embankments and around pointed palisades, towards the perimeter of the fortress. She launched from the tree, intending to follow him and call him back.

But the Mist called her name first.

She tried to ignore it. She shook her head, squeezed her eyes closed and drove blindly into the warm, damp air that burst to life around her. But the Mist could not be ignored. She felt her wings deaden with weight and tumbled head first into a snow bank.

Cawing, she beat snow from her wings. All around her, the snow began to thaw, peeling backwards like burning paper. Kenna fluttered to the top of a stone wall now clear of snow and waited. The Mist did not stop until the entire courtyard was as barren as the last day of autumn.

The bone woman peeled away from the swirling fog, hobbling through the Mist and straight for Kenna. "Not now!" Kenna hissed at her, flapping in agitation. The bone woman silenced her with the swipe of a hand, and no matter how Kenna tried, she could not make a single sound. Bound, mute, humiliated, she cowered against the stone.

The bone woman stopped, her dark eyes unblinking behind her snarl of hair. Then she changed. The wrinkles melted away. The colorless hair turned warm as honey, the black eyes as blue as summer skies, her skin as flawless as polished ivory. Kenna shrank away in disbelief. There was only one woman in all the Niflheim as beautiful as this: a woman who bore beautiful sons, and dreamed terrible dreams.

Frigg.

The vision only lasted moments, perhaps only a breath of a moment, and then the bone woman returned. "There is no more time," the hag wheezed, coughing and clutching at her chest. "I had thought with time—and distance—that my foolish son would find a woman to satisfy the curse, to thwart the prophecy. I had thought—but, no, I too am foolish. I too am trapped by this curse, and we none of us can be free until the curse is satisfied."

She drew several haggard breaths before continuing. "I tried to save him. It is apparent I have failed. You have failed. We have failed."

Kenna hung her head and opened her mouth to cry, but her bound throat would allow no sound. It was a voiceless, wrenching agony.

"There is nothing left, Kenna," the bone woman said, in a softer tone. "Nothing left, but for us to play our part. When the time comes, you must save him. When the time comes, I will help you. You must save my son. You owe him this. We owe him this."

Kenna nodded. She owed him this and more.

The pressure on her throat released, and she gasped for air like one close to drowning. The Mist curled away from her, leaving behind steaming stone and barren earth. The bone woman was gone.

Kenna turned and found the dragon slayer's daughter standing not far away, the potted rose bush in her arms, her jaw agape and eyes wide. Tosk burst from the opposite direction, past Kenna, and straight for Astrid. "I told you!" he shouted as he raced around her in circles. "I told you! Stupid, stupid!"

"Enough!" Kenna shrieked at him, enraged with them both. "Enough, Tosk! She can do nothing else: her Trial is at an end."

Astrid's face slackened in disbelief, while Tosk skidded to a halt and spun to face her, paws on his hips. "That's what I'm trying to tell you!" he shouted. "Baldur's doing something *stupid!*"

A sudden burst of wind ripped through the courtyard. It tugged at them, knocking Kenna off balance, throwing Astrid's hair across her face, tumbling Tosk across the ground as if he were nothing more than a leaf.

The bush in Astrid's arms shuddered, and the last of Frigg's roses ripped from the stem.

Kenna watched as the wind carried it away.

Baldur tumbled down the incline, away from Jar Rann, away from his home, his prison. He left it all behind. He left behind the hopes and the memories, and the squirrel and his stories. He left behind the nightmares he could never escape and the dreams he would never possess. He left behind the dragon girl he would never love and the bone girl he could never forget.

Baldur barreled into the woods, shoving saplings out of his way, hurdling frozen streams and fallen trees. He simply could not accept that he had brought others pain on his quest to save himself. Had he truly been so selfish? So narrowly focused? Not once had he considered the true fate of the girls he rejected. He had been running for so long, trapped in his own nightmare. He had forgotten that others suffered as well.

He was tired of running away—tired of hiding and waiting for his future to catch up with him. It all seemed so clear to him now. His future had always been in his own hands. He could not control which path he had been given, but he could control how he walked it and how many lives he dragged down with him.

This power had always been his. It was one thing even the curse could not take from him.

Baldur paused on the crest of a low hill. He looked back. He could not see Jar Rann, but he knew it was there. He looked forward. He could not see the Caves, but they too were there. For a moment, his fever cooled, his pulse slowed. He exhaled and shook himself, trampling snow beneath his paws.

He could go back. It was not too late. He could hope for a few more weeks, or days, or precious hours. Or he could go forward and face his future head on. He could wait for the smoke to find him, or he could summon the fire himself.

A bird twittered and flapped into the sky, probably disturbed by his rampage. He looked up and glimpsed a flash of brown as the hawk angled away from him. The sound of beating wings reminded him of raven wings. It reminded him of Kenna.

Baldur huffed and narrowed his eyes. He had already made the decision. He would not let someone else die for him, to settle some misguided debt. And he knew the raven. He knew that in the end she would not keep her promise. It had always been her way. She was a creature of rash moments, of emotional decisions.

No, in the end she would get herself killed—for him.

There was also the issue with the dragon slayer's daughter. She had no intentions of obeying him either. They were both of them stubborn and foolish.

He launched back on his hind legs and roared, louder and louder, until the icicles shook free of the trees and shattered against the frozen ground.

It was time.

Baldur plunged ahead and did not look back again. He knew what he needed to do. He knew what he wanted to do, what he was going to do. They were all the same.

He was going to summon the dragon.

TWELVE

The bear roared and the sound carried over the frozen ground, echoing in the frigid silence that cloaked the Ironwood Forest and the fortress beyond it. High in the ash tree, Munin lifted his beak to the sky.

"It is time," his brother said. "We must return; Odin will want to know that the end is near."

Munin sighed and stirred. "There is still hope," he disagreed in his soft, persuasive way. "Perhaps we can help."

"No," Hugin snapped, his feathers bristling. "Our duty is to watch and bring word. Odin must know of this. We will leave. Now." The wind seemed to grow colder, as if to confirm his intentions. Munin knew his brother's concerns without asking—that a storm was brewing and if they did not leave soon, they risked never leaving at all.

"She needs our help."

When Hugin nipped at him, he did not move to avoid the attack. "She is not our concern. She never has been. Think—do not feel."

"She is like us. Feel, do not think."

Hugin hissed and backed away, shaking his great beak side to side. "I will go, and you will join me. We will do our duty. It is the only right thing to do."

Munin's head drooped toward the branch he clutched with his feet. "Our duty is to serve our master," he murmured. "Watching is only one form of service. I will stay."

"If you stay, you will betray our Master! You betray me! Munin! We are brothers." This last part came out in softer tones, in tones laced with hidden meaning and many memories.

Munin lifted his head and met his gaze. "Believe me, brother. That is something I would never wish to do."

"Then come with me." Hugin leaned forward to bump his brother's shoulder with his beak.

Munin leaned into him, sighing softly. "I cannot," he whispered. "I will stay."

The other raven jerked away, as if bitten. He hissed and whipped his wings open. The bond between brothers ran deep, but the betrayal ran deeper. "Then you stay alone," he rasped. He launched from the tree and forged his way into the darkness.

Munin's heart ached with each stroke of his brother's wings, with each mile that came between them. He could not shorten that distance, because he could no more deny his convictions than Hugin could forsake his.

They were each bound to stay the course, no matter how far apart that course might drive them.

THIRTEEN

Kenna disappeared into the woods, cawing furiously.

The silence that followed was deafening. Astrid dropped the dead rose bush and turned on the squirrel, marching toward the ash were Tosk huddled against the roots, away from the bitter wind. Everything had become twisted awry, all her carefully made plans, her hopes and fears. "What has happened? Speak, squirrel, or I shall shake you until you do!"

Tosk bristled and lifted his head. "You will touch me on pain of death!"

"Do not tempt me!" Astrid snapped as she crouched down before him. "Now, speak! What has Baldur done?"

Tosk stared up at her, defiant, his nose quivering. One giant tear filled his eye and trailed down his cheek. He swiped at it with a paw. "He's gone to the dragon, that's what he's done," he wailed at long last. "It is all your fault, too. It is, do not deny it—"

"Where?" Astrid shouted. "Has he gone to the Caves?" If Baldur summoned the dragon, he would steal the last of her honor. It was she who should have found the dragon. It was the only way she could earn her father's respect and seek paltry justice for the girls in her village. If Baldur stole this from her—then everything she had done would have no purpose. She would never earn her father's respect, let alone her own. She groaned and tugged at her hair. Everything had gone wrong. It was all wrong.

This was not how it should end.

Her eyes snapped open and focused on some distant point. Nor would it end this way. Not if she could help it. There was still a way. It was a slight chance—a hopeless chance—but it was a chance all the same. She turned back to the squirrel, and when she spoke, she spoke with the authority of a dragon slayer's daughter.

"I have need of you, Tosk, and you will help me."

The squirrel bolted upright, barking at her. "I will not help *you*!"

"You will."

Tosk's head tipped to one side at her calm assurance. He tugged at his ear tufts and stared at her, hard and speculative. "*Why* will I help you?" he asked.

Astrid leaned down so that they were nearly nose to nose. "Because you want to help Baldur. And because if we succeed," she said, "it will make a glorious tale. Well worth repeating." The squirrel took to her words. She could see his thoughts plainly in his expression. He was intrigued. Annoyed. Excited. Nervous.

"We'll be helping Baldur?" he asked at long length. He twisted his whiskers around one finger, his tongue tucked in the corner of his mouth. His eyes gleamed with the prospect. "Glorious, you say?"

Astrid exhaled and smiled. "The most glorious tale ever told, my friend."

FOURTEEN

Kenna searched all through the day. She pressed on even though her wings trembled and threatened to fail her, even though her chest burned like fire and threatened to burn her from the inside out.

She could not find him.

The sun began to dip in the colorless sky. When she finally circled back toward Jar Rann, she found Baldur sitting just outside the eastern gate, head bent and shoulders drooping. Kenna's strength failed her and she plummeted to the earth into a bank of snow. She lay still, chest heaving with painful breaths, staring up at a pitiless sky.

Baldur's nose appeared, sniffing, and then his face. He fished her from the snow without speaking and turned to hobble back toward the fortress, with her tucked awkwardly under one arm. She did not stir until he entered the barren courtyard and paused, surveying the scene. The ground still steamed from the heat of the Mist the bone woman had brought.

"You have been busy," he said, as if he thought it had been her. He sounded ancient and weary. "Causing mischief, are you?"

"Are you?" she whispered back. She wiggled until he set her down on the still warm ground. She trembled and curled into herself. She longed to ask him about the dragon, but the words would not come. She feared that once she spoke them they would become true.

He dropped down beside her.

"He was not there," Baldur said as he lowered his head to his paws. He did not look at her but stared unseeing across the courtyard. "I called his name. I challenged him. Called him coward and worm and a dozen other terrible things."

And yet he was still alive, which could only mean one thing. But she did not say that. "That's not like you," she whispered instead. It must have pained him to say those things. It simply wasn't in his nature to call names, to instigate quarrels. He was not like her.

"He did not come." Baldur shifted, so that she could no longer see his face. "He would not come to me."

That is a good thing, she wanted to shout at him, but she knew he would not agree with her. Still, she rejoiced even as he agonized. She knew it was a hateful thing to do, to rejoice in another's suffering, but it meant he might live another day. She could not help herself.

A shout of alarm interrupted them. The sound was muffled but close. Baldur heaved himself from the ground and hurried to investigate. Kenna tried to follow, but her body still refused to cooperate. She squawked and flopped awkwardly across the ground.

She could tell now that it was Astrid who shouted, but she could not make out what the useless girl shouted about. Where was Tosk when she needed him! He would surely tell her all, and more. She forced herself to keep moving, dragging her exhausted body across the courtyard and toward the gate where Baldur had disappeared.

Wings fluttered above her. She craned her head and caught sight of a raven leaning over the wall, watching whatever happened beyond it. "What is it?" she shouted. "What do you see?" When Munin would not answer, she struggled with renewed determination, tottering toward the gate, toward the unknown, toward Baldur.

She stumbled out into the open. Baldur and Astrid stood side by side, both staring at the western sky that kissed the peaks of the high hills above the Caves. Kenna moved to the left, to see around them. The western sky was ablaze in color—crimson and orange color that stretched from one end of the horizon to the other, brilliant and terrible. The clouds curled like dragon fire, fringed in gold.

Munin dropped down beside her. He shoved his head beneath her wing and helped her stand. She felt his beak pressing against her throat. It made it difficult for her to swallow, for her to breathe.

"It is time," he whispered. "Kenna. The sky cannot lie."

The sky told a dreadful story, one Kenna had tried to keep untold for many, many years. But it seemed the story simply refused to be left untold. The sky told the truth, the terrible truth.

"The cave dragon is awake," Astrid said, her voice equal parts awe and fear.

Baldur spun, his large body knocking the girl to one side as he twisted around. Munin hissed and scuttled away, but it was Kenna that Baldur came for. He caught her in his mouth and and barreled for the fortress. Kenna fought against him, but he had caged her with his teeth. She was unharmed, merely trapped. Baldur did not stop until he shoved open the store room door and dumped her carelessly across it.

Kenna picked herself up, appalled and terrified at once. "What are you doing?" she cried. He had never been violent with her before, not even in the beginning when he had just cause for violence, when she first cursed him with his brutish body and cursed herself with this fragile but hideous bird frame.

"There are things I must say," he gasped, blocking the doorway and the light so that she could see nothing but him.

"There is nothing to say!" She flapped her wings at him. How she wished she had bound herself to a useful body, a lioness or even a wild boar—anything with teeth and tusks and strength—anything to remind him that now was the time to prepare for battle, not waste time with words.

"It's you, you know." Baldur ignored her protests, determined to not let her derail him from whatever it was he intended to say. "It's always been you." He huffed, his sides easing in and out as he took deep, laboring breaths.

Kenna hunched deeper into herself, wishing she could stop him. This was not the way it was meant to be. The store room felt suddenly close and stifling. She could not breathe.

"I would rather die a thousand deaths," he continued, his voice soft and barely discernable, even though they were alone and the room was utterly silent. "A thousand deaths, Kenna, than to live and love a hundred girls who are not you."

A sound escaped her that she did not mean to allow. It was agony. It was joy. It was so many things, and none of them right, none of them good.

"I do not blame you, Kenna, for what you did. I deserved it."

She moaned and shook her beak side to side. "You did not! I should never have tested you!"

"You had every right to test me," he replied. "I failed your test, and you, most bitterly. I thought myself a good man, but I was selfish. And proud. For that, I will always be sorry."

"You have nothing to be sorry for!" she insisted, desperate for this conversation to be over. At the same time, she hoped it never to end, that they might remain trapped in this moment forever.

"Yes," he said. "I do."

Then Baldur backed away and slammed the door on her, shutting her in darkness.

FIFTEEN

He felt free.

"It's always been you," Baldur said again and reveled in the weightlessness that accompanied honesty, but the thought of Kenna confined in that store room quickly cooled his fervor. He hurried away from the room, his heart light and heavy at once. It felt right to have spoken his heart; it felt wrong to have left her the way he did. It was her own fault, however, because he could not trust her.

He loved her.

But he did not trust her.

The conflicting emotions inside him seemed to get worse. He imagined them as two snakes in his belly. They felt alive inside him, waging a war on his own body. Baldur groaned and leaned against the side of the longhouse. Something was not right.

He blinked and shook his head, but his vision remained spotty and uncertain. There was not time for *this*—whatever this was. Fafnir was coming. The end was coming. He did not have time for anything but the dragon.

His body recoiled, wracked with pain. Baldur groaned and dragged himself to the shredded door of the longhouse. He pulled himself inside, his mouth agape with soundless cries. It felt as if every fiber of his body warred against the other parts. He was being torn apart from the inside out.

He fell to the floor, writhing, and wondered if this was how he would die: not at the hand of a dragon, but alone and helpless on the floor. It was not a death worth remembering.

Heat washed over him as darkness bore him away.

It was momentary. When he awoke, he knew something was wrong. He felt cold and exposed. Baldur shivered and stretched a paw toward the fire. A man's hand appeared before him. He stared at it, flexing pale human fingers, unable to comprehend who it belonged to. He pushed up into a seated positon to take stock of himself.

There was no bear, no fur or paws or sharp black claws.

He touched his face in disbelief, felt the roughness of a beard, but the smoothness of a human nose, a human brow. He barked a laugh.

After all this time, human again.

The laugh died within him. Human, just in time for the dragon to kill him. As a bear, he might have stood a chance. But as this? As a man, weakened and unsure of his arms and legs, he knew he would not stand a chance.

Baldur found his feet, took several unsteady steps, and then found a wall to lean against. No, he would not stand a chance but that did not mean he should lay around waiting. Everything he needed was here waiting for him, even after all this time— his clothes, his weapons, his memories.

He was thinner than he used to be. The clothes hung on him and the broad axe was covered in dust and dull from disuse. Yet his memories of being human felt vague but familiar, like a habit one cannot quite forget even after an eternity.

He only wished Kenna could see him now, but there was no time for that.

As the ground beneath his feet began to tremble, Baldur moved toward the longhouse doorway with purpose and confidence.

The dragon was coming.

SIXTEEN

Fafnir climbed over the palisade, like a snake slithering over the lip of its hole. The barricades were nothing to the cave dragon. He knew his own strength, knew each sinew and scale like a tree knew each branch and leaf. He was massive, the weight of ten bears, and covered in slime and moss from his long slumber.

He was ravenous.

The dragon twisted his angular face side to side as he surveyed the scene before him. He saw stone walls, wooden palisades and thatch roofed buildings. He saw a high tower, and a tree and a girl.

All these were nothing to him.

He had come for a bear, and before the night had ended, he would feast on bear or his name was not Fafnir the Glutton. Fafnir the Thief. Fafnir the Terrible. Pain stabbed his heart as he recited the names the humans had given him, the names to describe his deeds. This had not always been his life. Once he and his mate had lived in the mountains with their young hatchlings, secluded and safe. Dragons had not always been at war.

All that changed when the humans came with their snares and axes and razor-edged arrows. War was the handiwork of men and—when pressed—dragons were only too willing to comply. He returned hurt for hurt, death for death, until nothing remained but the monster the humans wished him to be. Then he hid himself in his caves to lose agony in sleep. He choked on a grief that still festered within him. None had dared to disturb his slumber, for more years than he could count. The bear would soon learn the folly of his indiscretion.

Fafnir roared and set fire to the thatch.

Some distance away, Tosk saw the spark that set fire to the fortress.

He skidded to a halt atop a small boulder, his nose lifted to the air. He sniffed, and as he did, his eyes widened. He smelled smoke, of course, and the distinctly acrid scent of dragon. Like most creatures in the world, a dragon had its own unique scent.

The human had betrayed him. By sending him on this silly errand, she intended to keep him away just when things were getting really interesting.

After all these years of waiting to set things to rights, he was going to miss *everything*.

Tosk launched from the top of the boulder and across a long line of smaller ones sticking out of the snow. As he went, he called that dragon girl every unkind name he could think of, which was rather a long list, as Tosk had suffered many injustices and knew just the right word for each and every one of them. In his haste, he slid off one of the smaller rocks and disappeared into a snow drift. He emerged, his fur frosted in snow, even more irate.

This, too, was the dragon girl's fault.

He clawed his way back onto the rock just as a second burst of fire roared to life on the plateau far above him.

The dragon had finally come. He wanted to return immediately to the fortress, but something held him back, a tugging at his conscience he did not want to hear. The girl had sent him to Sandfell for a reason. What if she was right? What if Baldur's life depended on him returning with the dragon slayer?

Even if it meant he missed out on *everything?*

Astrid stared at the dragon, for while she had seen many dragons, she had never seen one like him. This dragon must surely be one of the greats, with a body lithe like a fox but with the scaled armor of a lizard. The creature's wingless body was covered in moss but beneath the moss, his scales were the color of old coins.

Astrid gasped. She knew this dragon. The treasure thief. The woman eater.

"Have you seen what you came for, girl?" The voice was Baldur's. She did not bother looking at him, nor did she deny his accusation.

This was indeed the dragon she had come for. It was the dragon her father had hunted all her life, and half of his own. It was the dragon who had slaughtered Sigurd's first wife and caused endless misery—the dragon who would kill Baldur and end the Trials.

"Fafnir," she whispered.

Someone grabbed her and spun her about. Astrid gasped and recoiled. It was a man who had hold of her, a man in furs and hides too large for him. They stared at one another, her in confusion, and him with something akin to anger.

Or perhaps it was fear. The two were often the same.

The man's eyes were deep brown. She knew those eyes. "Baldur," she said, as if it did not surprise her in the least. Because it did not. She asked herself if she regretted her choice, now that a man stood before her and not a bear. But, no, her heart had not changed.

She did not—could not—love him.

"Well, you have seen your dragon," he told her roughly, his fingers squeezing her arm. "And now you will do what I ask, because you owe me that much."

When she did not argue with him, Baldur nodded and released her. "Kenna is in the store room," he said, hefting a massive double-edged axe against his shoulder. He moved away from her, toward the dragon. But he paused to look back. "Please, keep her there."

Then he turned and shouted the dragon's name.

Astrid muttered a prayer, that Tosk be fleet of foot and undistracted on his mission. Everything now depended on him.

SEVENTEEN

He still loved her after all she had done.

Kenna beat against the walls, against the door. She clawed at the thatch roof with her beak and talons and scrabbled against the hard-packed earth at the base of the walls. The bars of her prison were as unrelenting as the metals fashioned in the great forges. She could not contain her ecstasy any more than she could cope with her agony.

As a last resort, she summoned the Mist.

The bone woman came, as she had promised, walking through the Mist Door and into the blackness of the store room. Kenna's wings trembled from exhaustion, her head bobbing up and down as her muscles jerked. The bone woman saw her at once. "What are you doing in here?" She frowned and rapped her cane against the earth. "This is no time for your nonsense, bird."

"I am trapped!" Kenna scuttled away from the old one. "You promised to aid me. I need you now. It is time."

"Time," the bone woman murmured, in a loving way, as if she spoke of a familiar friend while Kenna spoke of a mortal enemy.

"Time!" Kenna hissed and beat her wings. "The dragon has come. My time is here. I must be released. I must—"

"You must what, raven-girl? You have failed him every step of the way. Your task was simple." The air shuddered. The bone woman melted away like wax before a flame, and Frigg appeared before her. Despite her beauty, something dark and haunted burned behind her eyes. When Frigg spoke again, she lifted her hands, claw-like, as if she wished to strangle Kenna. "Why could you not let him go?"

Kenna fell back, confused and alarmed that Baldur's mother had not come to give her aid as promised. Her pride chafed and burned, because she had done her part. She had given Frigg's son up. For years she had kept herself away from him, thrusting girl upon girl before his eyes. Beside them, with their braided hair and shapely limbs, she was a thing of horror.

Scavenger. Death-eater.

She gave him nothing but sharp words and dire warnings. What he had chosen to do with her unpleasant offerings was not her fault. "I cannot be blamed for his foolishness," she said, even as her heart swelled with the knowledge he still wanted her, after all these years—that nothing had changed his mind—not the bones, not the Trials, nor Frigg herself. Frigg had moved heaven and earth to change Baldur's destiny, but in the end he chose to embrace Fate rather than change himself for it.

I would rather die a thousand deaths, than to live and love a hundred girls who are not you.

Baldur had always been the best of them all, not because of any great feats, but because of his heart, his goodness. She could not say the same of herself. She had changed. How she had changed in her battle to save him! She was the bone girl no more. There was nothing of that creature left. She was raven, only.

"'The Raven falls,'" Kenna whispered. The time had finally come. "'All is lost or not lost.'"

Frigg shrank into herself, the bone woman once again. When she spoke, there were tears in her eyes. "'Will no one love my son?'" she whispered back. "'Ever by blood is Fate slated.'"

Kenna moved toward Baldur's mother, toward the one who had labored alongside her all these long years. She hunched at Frigg's feet, head bowed. "Release me," she begged. "It is time."

"It is time," the bone woman repeated. "But I am not here to release you, raven-girl. That power has always been your own. Only you can reclaim your former self. Only you can save my son."

Kenna lifted her head, her mind roaring under the barrage of her thoughts. "I cannot!" she cried. "I did not even know the curse I cast on us! I have tried, countless times, but to no avail. I cannot undo this curse!"

The bone woman knelt before her, her eyes dark and unseeing. "That," she said, half smile, half frown, "is because it was never your curse to cast. It was mine. The curse came from my hand. Not yours. I thought you would not let him go if I did not drive you away. I've seen the end, and one of you must die. I knew, that when that time came, my son's good nature would triumph. He would get himself killed—for you."

Kenna flinched. That hollow place inside her grew abruptly endless. She would not believe this story, not after all this time. All these years she had agonized and punished herself, all because of this thing she had done. And now! If what Frigg said was true? She had wasted her time and her life. She would have done so many things differently. She would have—

"Save my son," the bone woman whispered.

The tempest inside her stilled.

That was the one thing Kenna would not have done differently. No matter what Frigg had done, no matter how cruel her deception, she had done it to protect her son. Kenna could not fault her for that. Perhaps it was the only noble thing the woman had ever done.

"I will save him," she croaked, nearly choking on the words, on words that wanted to lash out and return hurt for hurt. But there was no time for that. "Not for you. For him."

Because she loved him, too. It did not matter that he was beast and she bird, that sky and earth hung between them. She loved him and he loved her.

In spite of everything, this had not changed. The Mist swelled, and Kenna closed her eyes to embrace it.

EIGHTEEN

Baldur lifted his shield before him with his other arm outstretched wielding his broad axe.

Fafnir snaked over the jagged palisade, his nostrils flared as he touched the Mist-warmed ground and sniffed the air. "I smell him on you, tiny man," the dragon hissed, smoke curling from between his teeth. Baldur braced himself as the stench of death and sulfur struck him. Around them, portions of Jar Rann were already burning. "Where are you hiding him? Where is the bear?"

"I am not hiding him," Baldur ground out. He lowered the shield and bared his teeth over the top of it. "I am him."

Fafnir laughed. It was the sound of rock grating over rock, of mountains moving and seas upheaving. "What magic is this?" he asked as he continued to move forward, like a cat haunting a mouse. "What treachery? Do you think me a fool?"

Baldur eased to the left, countering the dragon's moves. "No," he said, "I think you are a pig and a killer, but not a fool."

"Ah," breathed the dragon. "Now I recognize you, bear-man. Such cheek for one so weak."

"Do not let appearances fool you, dragon. There is more to man than meets the eye. We are capable of much more than filling a dragon's stomach."

The dragon snapped his jaw shut as he curled around the ash tree, one leg lifting to lean against the tree as he lifted himself higher. "Do not be fooled by delusions, bear man. Do you think only dragons are a plague upon the earth? Look to your own history—man destroys. Man slaughters. Man devours. Man should be swiped from the earth. For every dragon you have slain, I will reap my revenge ten-fold." A small burst of flames caught the lower limbs on fire.

Heat flared through Baldur, that this beast thought so much of his own lair but so little of another's. "I cannot speak for all of history, but I can speak for today. I speak for myself!" He smashed his axe against the side of the shield. The sound of the impact echoed away and back again. "Today we are destined to meet in battle and at the end of it, one of us shall die."

"Resigned to your fate then, are you, bear-man?"

In that moment, Baldur could have thought of any hundred things—of his childhood, his mistakes, his unfulfilled dreams. But Baldur thought only of a raven-clad bone girl. Every moment in his life, since the day his mother had dreamed that prophecy, had been a series of moves and countermoves all tugging him toward this inescapable place, to this one moment in time.

This had always been where he was meant to come, but did that mean he welcomed it? Was he at long last resigned to his fate?

"Are you deaf, little man? Are you ready to die?"

"I have had a long time to contemplate that question," Baldur said, hefting his axe. "I know my destiny. So tell me, dragon, do you know yours?"

"A dragon needs no destiny."

Baldur braced himself, the fear and adrenaline coursing through him. In this moment, he was very much alive. "That seems unfair," he said between clenched teeth. "Let me share mine with you."

Then, Baldur drew back his arm and rushed forward.

Man and dragon collided in an explosion of fire.

Astrid checked the store room door to be sure it was secure. She would do her duty quickly so that she might get back to the dragon. All within was silent. She paused, ear pressed to the door. It was like that bird to hide, out of spite, just when Astrid needed to know exactly where she was.

"Hello, bird?" she called.

Even the wind did not answer her. She quickly scouted the exterior of the store room, but there were no telling cracks in the walls. She even hefted herself onto the roof and scoured the thatch, but found no cranny through which the bird might escape.

"Have your sulk then!" she called through the roof. She hoped the bird heard her, and that it irked her exceedingly.

Behind her, fire crackled and burned.

Astrid trotted across the ridge pole of the store room and hauled herself up the more steeply slanted roof to the longhouse. As she pulled herself over the top, she saw the ash tree burning. She could see the mossy back of the dragon, bucking up and down as it chased something darting around its feet. She shrugged out of her bulky overcoat but left her sword slung against her back, exposing her bare arms to the cold. She withdrew a long dagger from the sheath strapped to her thigh. Then, she slid down to the edge of the roof.

She could not see Baldur.

The dragon roared and spit another ball of fire toward the stables. Baldur appeared from beneath the belly of the dragon. He rolled clear of the beast, his axe swinging out and behind him so that he slashed at Fafnir's hind leg as he came to a crouch. The dragon howled and staggered against the tree. It creaked and groaned beneath him.

"Enough of your games, little man!" shouted the dragon. "Are you bear or mouse? I shall crush you, and grind you, and spit out your bones! I shall—"

Baldur delivered another blow to the dragon's softer underbelly, and then tucked himself in and rolled beneath the dragon, only to emerge and attack from a different front.

He was using the monster's bulk and slow reflexes to his advantage.

But all of his blows were mere annoyances to the dragon. He was only enraging it. Astrid crouched on the edge of the roof, biding her time, waiting for Baldur to move the dragon into position. If he could just drive him back about two yards—

As Baldur darted beneath him again, Fafnir changed tactic and spun his body around, his tail writhing out to catch the man unawares. Baldur fell with a soundless thud, and although he managed to tumble out of Fafnir's reach, he lost his shield. As Baldur found his feet, the dragon shattered the shield beneath his right leg, rending it to pieces. Baldur staggered backward, axe held in front of him. He was clearly growing weary.

Fafnir approached cautiously, a sound like roaring rapids erupting from inside his throat. It was a laugh, Astrid realized. Fafnir knew that Baldur was no match for him. There was hardly any sport in this contest. Baldur had courage, and quick reflexes, but he was no dragon slayer.

There would be no time to wait for Tosk.

"Fool!" the dragon spat. "Did you really think you stood a chance against me?" He lifted his head, mouth open to set fire to the man below him. He moved into range. Astrid launched from the side of the roof, dagger in both hands. The blade slid into Fafnir's eye like a spade into churned soil and the dragon screamed and buckled. Astrid clung to the dagger, as blood and eye fluid poured over her hands. Her body smacked against the dragon. She could feel the blistering heat as Fafnir poured his fire into the sky.

But the dragon yet lived, and he knew she was there. Bellowing, he moved to crush her against the side of the longhouse. Astrid released her grip on the blade and slid down the dragon's neck, dropping clear just as Fafnir smashed through the longhouse, taking half the roof and structure down with him. She tried to scramble clear, on all fours like an animal, but something hit her from behind, and she fell into darkness.

NINETEEN

A raven entered the store room.

A woman left it.

Kenna walked out on two legs, on two human legs. She leaned against the side of the building, trying to find her footing. It felt so wrong, without wings to keep her balance, without dark feathers cocooning her own heat against her body. She had become accustomed to the freedom of the skies, to the comfort of her wings.

Here she was, at the moment of crisis, bound to the earth. She still wore the feathered costume she had used to deceive Baldur, to test his good nature. She had come before him, then, as an ugly old woman, clothed in disgusting rags and feathers. Of course he had not seen her for herself. Of course he would turn her away.

It had been a foolish mistake, one that had cost them not in gold but in years. Perhaps the curse had not come from her hand, but she had paved the way for Frigg's desperate decision.

She staggered around the side of the store room, tears burning behind her eyes. Now there were no years left to waste. There was no more time—it was now or not at all. She had to find a way to save him because no one else could do it. She had no weapons, no powerful curses. She was but a simple bone girl, toying with tricks and dabbling in mists. She had nothing useful to offer. Nothing but herself.

Perhaps she could distract the dragon long enough so that *something* might happen. Baldur might strike a killing blow. Astrid might finally do what she had been brought here to do—end the curse. Frigg might finally discover a way to change the course of her Prophecy.

Kenna did not know how it would end. She only knew that blood needed to be shed.

"Ever by blood," she whispered. And she would make sure it was raven blood—not Baldur's—that was shed this day.

She could hear the dragon roaring. She could feel the heat of his fires and the tremble of his steps. She rounded the side of the stables and stopped, horrified by what she found. Half the fortress burned, the longhouse almost entirely gone, crushed to smoldering ruins. The dragon wrapped himself around the ash tree, roaring into the sky.

Kenna caught sight of movement beyond him. A man appeared, smeared in blood, hefting an axe. At first, she did not recognize him; it had been such a long time. But her memories did not desert her for long. She knew that face better than she knew her own.

Baldur had already found a way to break the curse.

For the first time in nearly a decade, they were human again. Both of them.

Yet the space between them yawned as endless as ever. It was still a void she could never hope to cross. She watched as Baldur lifted his axe above his head and the dragon turned to greet him with fire and teeth.

"No!" she cried and stumbled into the courtyard. "You are here for me, dragon!"

The monster ignored her. They both did. Kenna resorted to the only weapons she possessed: her tricks. She called the Mist, asked it to waft across the courtyard, to surge up and over the dragon as if it were a creature itself. Fafnir paused, confused, as the Mist Dragon coiled alongside him.

"What treachery is this?" he hissed.

"Mine!" Kenna called. Fafnir turned to face her. "This is your true destiny, dragon. You have come here today for me. The bones have spoken."

Both man and dragon stared at her, the dragon in disbelief and the man in horror. Kenna forced herself not to meet the man's gaze, so she would not have to die with the memory of his betrayed face before her eyes. She was not betraying him, not this time.

Fafnir swiped at the Mist Dragon, which split like smoke before him. It was, after all, only a trick. The dragon bellowed, enraged. He spun on her, knocking Baldur to the ground as he slithered around the tree. "Stupid girl!" he snarled. "You are no match for me either."

Kenna willed herself to stand firm, even though her insides turned to liquid. "Perhaps not, but I am no trifle either," she challenged. "Why not test me? This man is nothing, no match for you. I am. Test me."

She would be the final Trial.

The dragon coiled toward her, through the mist. Kenna caused the Mist Dragon to drop on him from above and blinded him in the cloud. She darted to the south, scrambled over a stone embankment and ducked for cover. Fafnir's fire split the mist, causing it to writhe and settle.

"No one is match for me!" he snarled. "Come out, bird girl, and face your death. I can already taste you."

Kenna shuddered and braced herself for what must come next. The end had finally come. She exhaled and lifted her head, preparing to rise.

"Kenna!" Baldur bellowed in horror. "Kenna! No!"

But she had already left her hiding place, trying to refashion the Mist as she did, but the Mist balked, weakened by the fire. The time for tricks was at an end. The dragon leered at her as she climbed back onto the rock embankment, arms extended to either side, feathered cloak falling away like a sick joke compared to the wings that had once been hers. Baldur thundered toward them, shouting, but he would be too late.

As the dragon head descended, Kenna closed her eyes. At long last, it was time to end the Trials.

TWENTY

Astrid shoved away the debris pinning her to the ground, coughing, one hand at the back of her head to stem the flow of blood. She rose to her feet and staggered until she found her balance. Around her, the fortress burned. She took in the scene in an instant.

Baldur, racing across the courtyard. The dragon, descending to consume. A girl in a raven cloak, waiting with wings outspread.

What on earth had she missed?

She surged forward, unsure what she was supposed to do, but when Astrid reached for her sword, she did not find it strapped to her back. Frantic, she scoured the wreckage around her. Her hands were shaking when she threw aside a wad of singed thatch and found her sword lying in the dirt. As soon as her fingers curled around the handle, calm seemed to spread through her. Her hands grew still and sure. The familiar weight comforted her. She turned and began to race toward Fafnir.

The dragon plunged for the raven girl.

An ink black form shot through the sky, dropping like an arrow for the dragon. Astrid skidded to a halt as the raven attacked Fafnir's good eye. The dragon screamed, coming to his knees, probably blinded by the attack. As he snapped his head to the side, Fafnir flung the raven across the courtyard. The bird smacked against the stone tower with a sickening thud and fell to the ground mere yards from Astrid.

The raven fell and did not move.

It was Munin.

Astrid turned her back on the bird. There was nothing to be done for him now. Fafnir staggered all over the courtyard, spewing smoke and fire. He slipped on the edge of a stone wall and lost his balance, thundering to the ground and rolling downhill, over other staggered embankments.

Astrid did not think. She ran.

Her legs pumped, fueled by years of training, by the adrenaline coursing through her veins, by destiny calling her name. This was why she had come. This was what she meant to do. She shouted as she chased after the dragon, leaping from one outcropping to the next, until she was nearly upon him. Her boots launched off the last rock wall, her sword clutched in both hands. Fafnir did not have time to deflect her attack.

He could not even see her coming.

Astrid drove the blade into his scaled flesh, hoping that the momentum of her attack would give her the strength she needed to drive the blade through the armor to the dragon's heart.

It was not. Her heart sank when Fafnir writhed beneath her, the blade merely six inches into his golden-scaled hide. The dragon bucked, trying to dislodge her. She threw every ounce of her strength into the task at hand, but the blade would sink no further.

Someone bellowed her name. She looked up to see Baldur nearly upon her, his axe lifted over his head. She leapt backward as she realized his intent. The prince brought the axe down on its side and smashed into the sword handle as if he wielded a hammer and not an axe. With one single blow, he drove the blade to its mark. Fafnir's fire sputtered and faded. Still, the dragon shuddered, even as his death throes weakened and his massive head fell back, smashing an abandoned cart to splinters.

At last, the dragon lay still.

Astrid looked up at Baldur, her breathing ragged and frantic. He stared back at her. Blood smeared his face and beard. Time, ever spinning, seemed to finally stop. A laugh burst from her throat—a laugh at once incredulous, ecstatic, and hysterical. "Your brother will be proud of that blow!" she exclaimed.

Baldur exhaled loudly and slid backward, off the belly of the dragon. He propped his axe over his shoulder. "These days, Thor finds little pleasure in the feats of others," he retorted dryly. He looked to the sky, his chest heaving with labored breaths. Then he looked to her and smiled.

Astrid would have smiled back, but a sudden shout rent the uncanny stillness the dragon had left in his wake. Her eyes fluttered closed as her heart dropped to the pit of her stomach, the fleeting thrill of their victory dashed in but a single moment. It was happening again.

"What have you done?" the newcomer exclaimed.

She knew that voice.

She tensed as her father rode toward them on the back of his horse, a beautiful roan as temperamental as he was. Sigurd swung from the back of the roan and dropped to the ground before the horse had even come to a halt. He ran toward them, only to collapse to his knees, body arched back as he bellowed in rage.

Astrid slid down beside Baldur. "This is Sigurd," she told him, in a hushed voice. "The dragon slayer. I think we have angered him."

Baldur shot her an annoyed look. She realized that this much was already apparent. She did not know how to explain it to him. There would be time for that later. She moved forward, covered in the blood of their mortal enemy.

"Father, I have avenged you," she said, but her words lacked conviction. She knew what was about to happen. "I have killed the dragon who consumed your first wife. Your beloved."

Sigurd lifted his head, his face twisted and unpleasant. "You have robbed me of my revenge!" he shouted back. "Worthless girl!" He launched to his feet, arm drawing back as he prepared to strike her. Astrid had already turned away, her shoulder hunched to protect her head against the coming blow.

She was accustomed to such anger.

Baldur caught Sigurd's fist before it fell. "You will not touch her," he said through his teeth, shoving backward as her father struggled to free himself. "This girl has done me a great service. She will always be beneath my protection. I am Odin's son, and you will listen to me."

"I should have left her to die when she was born!" Sigurd snarled. The blow struck as harshly as his fist would have. She felt the familiar walls rising, the familiar apologies darting to the tip of her tongue. "I always knew the child would haunt me, the child I never wanted—"

Baldur punched him. Astrid stared at him, surprised. She could tell by the look on his face that he felt little sorrow over it. Sigurd reeled backward, cursing. "You are a fool," Baldur said, the weariness apparent in his voice. "And you are not welcome here. This girl owes you nothing. She is free to come or go as she pleases. You will not touch her again. If I hear you have caused her grief, of any sort—" He left the threat unfinished.

He was a son of Odin. He did not need to say more.

It had been a long time since any man stood up for her. No one dared challenge her father, not when he protected them from the dragon pestilence. She understood her father's anger, understood that it grew from pain and fear, not hate. By slaying the dragon on her own, she had made him look weak. It had not been her intention.

But she could not undo it. Nor would she wish to. "I am sorry," she began, but Baldur sliced a hand in her direction.

"You owe him no apology," he said with authority. "You have done no wrong. You raised her, dragon slayer, and she has become what you raised her to be. Do not blame her for that."

Sigurd turned his gaze on her. She recognized that, in this moment, he could not stand to face this. He was too angry, too broken. He still ached over the loss of his first wife. Astrid dipped her head and took a step back, indicating that she desired no response from him. She wished them to part in peace. Her father said nothing when he left, but Astrid found this a good thing. She did not need him to say anything.

She had not slain the dragon for him.

Astrid reached into her pocket and pulled out the dragon rune. She held it tightly in her fist and considered giving it to Baldur, as a token. But the idea unsettled her. She did not wish to part with it, not even for a son of Odin. After all, she had not slain the dragon for him either.

Sometimes a woman had things to prove to herself.

As she thought about her scars, Astrid's hand moved of its own accord as if to cover the offensive reminders. She froze and forced her hand to lower back to her side. She smiled fiercely.

This day, she was proud of her scars.

TWENTY - ONE

Kenna sat at the base of the stone tower, Munin's broken body cradled in her arms. She did not understand what had happened—why he had done it—why he had sacrificed himself in order to spare her. She had always been the one destined to fall.

Why had he interfered?

Was it because they were alike? Ravens, watchers, servants? She did not know. In all honesty, she did not wish to know. She only knew that he no longer moved and she could not feel his breath.

Kenna rocked back and forth, consumed with emotions too violent for her weary spirit to handle. She had seen Baldur leap to Astrid's aid. How quickly he defended her, the way a man should when he loved a woman! He had sworn his love to her, but Frigg had been correct that Kenna was not right for him. She did not have it in her to be the noble wife of a prince. In all her years of trying, she had never been able to save him.

In the space of a few weeks, Astrid had changed everything. Of course a dragon slayer would be the one to save him. Of course he should fall for that woman. If Kenna was honest with herself, she had known this from the moment she saw Astrid rising in the mist, dragon slayer and monster. The girl had slain the dragon and claimed the hero.

It had always been meant to happen.

The gulf between them had not narrowed with the death of the dragon. The only noble thing she could do was let him go—let him go for a better future. The time had finally come for her to leave Jar Rann.

It had been her home and prison for too long. Her heart shriveled at the mere thought of leaving. Kenna wept soundlessly as she managed to find her feet, her body turning to shield her from the unfolding event she could no longer watch.

She was sick of watching.

Her steps were uneven as she made her escape around the crumbling tower, toward the nearest gate. She clutched Munin's lifeless body to her chest, crying as much for him as for herself. Her only hope was that she might escape unseen, without any more pain. She could not handle more.

The dragon was dead and the curse lifted. Baldur was safe.

She had no reason to stay.

Her spirit should feel light, now that she was released from her bondage, but the weight only seemed to multiply, until the weight of Munin in her arms was more than she could carry. She stumbled to her knees, trying to keep hold of him, but the raven writhed out of her grasp. Kenna startled. Was he not truly dead? How was the raven so strong in his near-death state? But the raven wasn't moving to rise. Instead, he was changing.

Kenna sat back in the snow as the raven became a man not much older than her, dressed in black, skin as pale as the snow. His skin was smeared with blood, too much blood. She felt his throat, his silky black hair caught in her fingers, but the pulse barely quivered against her touch. She cradled his head in her lap and wished she did not have to witness his death.

She had seen enough sorrow for two lifetimes.

A shrill squawk lifted her head, in time to see a raven tumbling toward her, fluctuating between bird and man as it approached. Hugin clung to his man-self and dropped to his knees, skidding up against her and the dying watcher. He pulled his brother into his arms, his mouth parted in a silent cry.

Kenna quickly withdrew, leaving them alone. The loss was not hers. She had no right to be here.

The familiar bark of a squirrel echoed from the forest moments before Tosk barreled out of it, his fur as red as the blood now staining the snow. He skidded to a halt mere feet from them. "Have we missed *everything?*" he cried as he pranced in frantic circles, his paws full of his ears, his cheeks, and his tail. He could not seem to stand still. Behind him, the Mist spilled from the forest.

"Yes," Kenna said, her voice weak and foreign to her ears, her eyes on the Mist and not Tosk. "I fear you have."

The squirrel burst into tears, hiding his face in his tail as he wept. He abruptly froze and looked up, horrified. His paws dropped to his rather pronounced midsection. "My stores," he whispered. "That wretched dragon is burning *all* my food!" He bolted across the snow, toward the burning fortress, howling in dismay about the loss of his hidden stashes.

The bone woman hobbled out of the Mist, her hair snarling on the wind as she approached. Behind her, a man separated from the shadows, a man with broad shoulders and scars from countless battles. The man lifted his head as he approached, one eye concealed behind a knotted bandage. Kenna ducked her head in deference to her master.

Odin. The Raven King had finally come.

"My son?" Frigg cried as the Mist pooled upward in a straight line, as if it had hit an invisible wall. Frigg and Odin hovered just inside it, present but not. "What have you done? You should not be here!" she accused, her hands reaching out, claw-like. Odin stilled her with a touch on the shoulder, but his single eye sought Kenna's face for the truth.

Kenna exhaled, trying to find control. "He lives. Your son lives," she said.

"But how? The raven must fall—" The words died on her lips as Frigg noticed the two brothers in the snow, one bleeding out and the other keening in sorrow. Her eyes shifted to Kenna. "What have you done?"

It stung, that her life had been valued lower than all others but Kenna kept this pain to herself. It was not within the servant's power to choose his type of servitude. It was his to obey. "He interfered," she said. "I was ready. I was all but dead, and then he—he—"

Odin took a step forward, the mist curling around his boots as he settled them in the thawing snow. "I have always feared for Munin," he said, his voice deep and resounding like echoes in a cavern. "He does not think."

"He only feels," Hugin whispered, his dark head bowed over his brother's. Odin's eye lifted from the brothers to something above Kenna's head. She spun, skittish as a newborn colt, and staggered deep into the snow, further from the group. Baldur and Astrid jogged away from the burning fortress, toward them. Baldur moved as if to approach her, staring, but Kenna averted her gaze, her arms wrapped around her trembling body. Even without looking, she knew when he stopped.

Frigg was murmuring his name, over and over again, as if reciting some ancient mantra, when in reality it was merely her mother's heart speaking when it had no words. "I don't understand," she whispered, tears streaming down her wrinkled cheeks. "Baldur, my son, I don't understand."

Odin reached for her hand, and she became his beautiful wife in an instant. "Perhaps," he said, a little sternly, "you did not see what you thought you saw."

"I know what I saw!" Frigg muttered, petulant. Her finger jabbed toward Kenna. "I saw the raven fall."

Odin sighed and took her finger, lowering it until it pointed not at Kenna but at the brothers. "There is more than one raven in the Niflheim," he murmured and slanted his eye toward the Watchers, his expression troubled and hurt. "The trouble with prophecies is that they are often misunderstood. A raven fell, but not the one you intended. Our son will die, as all men do. But not today."

He exchanged a look with his youngest son, one that Kenna felt was rather long overdue. While Frigg had been busy meddling and making matters worse, Odin had been strangely absent. It made little sense to her, but he was the Raven King and had many duties to occupy his time. Who was she to judge that which she could not understand? Perhaps the idea of losing his son had been so great he could only cope by distancing himself from the pain.

"The raven still lives," Baldur said, from where he had crouched in the snow, one hand on Hugin's shoulder. He glanced up, toward his father. "There is yet hope."

Odin nodded, slowly, as he contemplated. "It is a long journey, but if he can be brought to me, perhaps he can be saved."

Kenna opened her mouth, ready to do her duty once again. After all, it was her fault that Munin had fallen in the first place. But someone else spoke first.

"I will take him."

Astrid stepped forward, her arms bare, her braided hair a mess around her face. She clutched a bloody rag to the base of her skull, but she stood firm, chin lifted. "I will take him," she repeated. "I have long wanted to see the giants of the far north. Are they as terrible as dragons?"

Kenna's fingers curled into fists. The dragon slayer's daughter was going to steal even this from her. Was there nothing left for her in all the world?

Odin smiled at Astrid, his one eye glinting. "Ah, the dragon girl," he said. He inclined his head. "It seems I owe you a debt of thanks. I would be honored to receive you in my house." When Frigg said nothing, her lips lost in silent mutterings as she still gnashed over all that had happened, Odin moved his hand to rest it on the woman's shoulder.

Frigg looked up. "We would be honored," she said, but the shadows in her gaze clouded what should have been a joyous moment. Kenna found that she ached for her. They had both wasted so many years trying to avoid this day, only to have it whisked out of their grasp and turned upside down.

But not in a bad way. Baldur lived.

She had not been the one to save him, but that did not really matter in the end. Kenna repeated that to herself, over and over in her mind, even as she shuffled backward, longing to disappear before anyone noticed her absence. She need not have worried, however, for everyone was preoccupied. Astrid and Hugin prepared a makeshift sling with two sturdy branches and a hide strung between them. Baldur and Tosk filled packs with supplies for the journey. Odin held his wife's hand and murmured to her as she tottered on the brink of her sanity, her form darting back and forth between the bone woman and beautiful Frigg. When they turned and disappeared into the Mist, Kenna knew that it was time.

She was no longer needed.

Kenna turned and slipped into the forest, already forgotten. Her story would never be told, not even by Tosk, who loved nothing more than a thrilling tale of betrayal and loss. Besides, he had missed everything—all the important parts, anyway. She forged her way into the frozen forest, all but running.

It was time to leave the past behind her, time to face a future raw with uncertainties, a future that had not yet been foretold. She was done with bones. She no longer wanted to look forward.

She only wanted to forget.

TWENTY - TWO

Baldur returned from the fortress, a pack of food and water skins slung over his back. Tosk sat on his shoulder, pestering him with questions he had no intention of answering. Not yet. Astrid was busy lashing the wounded Watcher to the sling, while Hugin assisted. Baldur cast his eyes about. His father and mother were gone.

Kenna was gone as well.

His heart plummeted to the pit of his stomach. He slung the pack from his shoulder and thundered down the incline. Tosk yelped and tumbled to the ground. "Where is she?" he demanded. "Where has she gone?"

Astrid looked up, her face flushed with exertion. "Who?" she asked as she swiped sweat from her brow. Her expression cleared abruptly. "Oh, the raven." She shrugged one shoulder, indicating she neither knew nor cared.

Hugin shot him a dark look. Considering the circumstances, he probably wished Kenna were the one strapped to the sling, clinging to life like autumn's last leaf to the ash tree. "We are ready to leave," he said, his voice clipped, the words sharp like the squawk of the raven-tongue. "There is no time to play her games. Are you coming with us, Odin-son?"

Baldur spun in a circle, his eyes straining to find the form of a girl in the endless mounds of snow stretching away into the forest. He searched the ground near him, but there had been many feet trampling through the snow. He finally found a sole set of tracks leading toward the forest. He broke into a jog, ignoring the shouts that followed after him.

How could she leave like this? After everything they had been through? After everything he had said to her? When he caught her—if he caught her—he was going to slap her silly.

And then kiss her senseless, if she would allow it. By all that froze and burned, he had waited long enough to do it. It could not end this way. It simply could not.

Astrid watched as Baldur disappeared into the forest. Tosk flipped her leg with his tail as he bounded up to her, fussing to himself. She glanced at him. "Are you not going to follow them?"

"Is it any business of yours?" he asked, clearly upset with her for some reason.

Astrid stared down at him, his feelings of no consequence to her. She had never felt many kind thoughts for the meddlesome creature. The fact that he was still a meddlesome creature, after all that had happened, bothered her. She frowned. "Are you a man as well?" she asked, her tone nearly as accusing as his had been.

Tosk lifted himself up on his back legs and planted his paws on his hips. "I am a *squirrel!*" He said it as if being a squirrel were the most honorable and enviable thing in the world and she were a dunce for not knowing it.

Astrid felt a smile tug at her lips, but she suppressed it. The rascal was many things, but "humble" was not one of them. She inclined her head in a show of thanks. "It was good of you to bring my father," she said. "Although he arrived much too late."

Tosk blinked at her and relaxed his posture. "I know," he agreed with a sigh. If he caught her gentle jibe, he ignored it. "You owe me a full report, dragon girl, but later. I'm going to—ahem, find something to eat." He bounded away from her but not toward the fortress. Rather, he hurried after Baldur. She watched until his red fur disappeared into the snow mounds.

She turned back to Hugin. "How soon can we be off?" she asked.

She was ready to leave this place. In all her life, she had never been more than few miles from Sandfell. The world felt large and welcoming, even though their mission was one of sorrow and urgency.

"There is nothing keeping us here," the raven man replied, in an unpleasant tone. She frowned at him but said nothing. She hoped he did not plan to take his ire out on her for the entirety of their journey. She had no idea how far their travels would take them or how long it would last, but now that she was free of her father, she had no inclinations to exchange him for another sullen companion.

Astrid shouldered her pack but kept her irritation to herself. After all, today was not a day for wallowing in one's troubles. Today was a day for reveling in victories and looking forward to those that would soon come. Who knew what adventures she would encounter in the land of the giants while performing the bidding of the great Raven King!

She brushed her finger tips over her scars, caressing them. Then, she yanked on her fur mittens and moved to assist the raven man with the sling they had constructed. It would be heavy, but she had never suffered from a lack of hard work.

Hugin glowered at her before turning to pick up his half of the sling. They set off in silence, yet Astrid found herself smiling at her companion's stiff back. Today was a day for reveling. So she would revel and dream.

The dragon-slayer's daughter was finally leaving home.

Tosk raced to keep up. He leapt from boulder to tree to boulder, voicing his outrage in sharp barks. But Baldur ignored him, yards ahead, smashing through small trees and snow drifts as if he were still a bear. His voice echoed through the frozen wood.

He shouted the raven's name.

Tosk caught hold of a swinging limb that Baldur flung back toward him, using the momentum to fling himself into the air and high into the trees. He raced across icy limbs, from tree to tree, until he had passed Baldur and left him behind.

He caught sight of the silly raven girl hiding behind a large oak. Tosk slid to a stop, shouting and pointing. Baldur's eyes darted toward him and then slanted in the direction Tosk indicated. Kenna, realizing he had betrayed her, bolted in another direction. But Baldur caught sight of her and overtook her with little effort. When she refused to stop, he tackled her from behind and plunged them both into the snow.

Tosk scampered to the nearest tree, jumping from limb to limb until he hung directly over them. They were both sitting in the snow, shouting and waving their arms like fledglings screaming for breakfast. Tosk rolled his eyes and tucked in to wait it out.

"Go back to your dragon girl!" Kenna shouted, her voice high-pitched and hysterical. "It's what you should do! It's what you should want."

"It is *not* what I should want!" Baldur shouted back. "Odin's Eye! Do not put words into my mouth, Kenna. I've lived without speech long enough, and I will be hanged if I let anyone speak for me again. She's gone by now, anyway. And I care not if she is."

"Well, you should," Kenna sputtered and picked herself up, shaking snow from her skirts as she stepped back. Baldur caught her by the ankle and yanked so that she came back down beside him. Tosk chuckled to himself. This was just like old times, like the really old times, before things all went bleak.

Before things went all raven and bear, and dragons and curses.

He leaned down a little closer as Kenna beat at Baldur with her fists, crying and shouting all at once. She always did know how to make a scene. It might not make for the best retelling, but he could always gloss over some parts. He had missed so much already he was going to have to extrapolate quite a bit as it was.

Tosk thought of the coin-colored dragon and lost himself in a day dream.

TWENTY - THREE

Kenna's hands shook. She was so angry—so hurt—so confused.

Why couldn't he just leave her alone? Did he not understand she was trying to help him? She swung at him again, but her half-hearted attack did not even elicit a response from him.

"Why are you fighting this?" Baldur finally asked. He caught hold of her flailing fists and held them firm. "It's over, Kenna. Leave it be. It's time to for us to move on."

"We cannot move on! I cannot live like this," Kenna cried. "Don't you understand? She saved you, Baldur. *She broke the curse.* Not me." Her voice dropped to a whisper. "She is the girl for you. It never could have been me."

She heard a gasp above them and glanced up to Tosk staring at her, a stricken look on his furry face. Yes, she wanted to tell him, those are your words. Perhaps it was time he learned the power words carried and the devastation they could cause.

She had certainly learned as much.

"Kenna, she did not break the curse," Baldur whispered back, clearly unaware of Tosk. "I did. You did. My mother said the curse would fall if I loved a girl and she loved me in return. We satisfied the curse when we stopped running from ourselves. You cannot punish yourself over something that may have or may not have happened. Redemption is not something you earn. Like forgiveness, it is something you are given."

This struck deep.

"Look at me!" Kenna said, hating that she sounded as desperate and hysterical as his poor mother. She stared at him, unsure how to express herself, how to tell him that things had changed. The years had changed them. The hurt had changed them. He was older now, no longer a dreamy-eyed boy with visions of making the world a better place. He had crow's feet around his eyes, premature grey streaking his temples.

He had so many scars.

And she looked worse, a scarecrow with hollows beneath her eyes and blue veins standing out on her rail-thin arms. "I am not the same girl you knew. We are both different. We cannot simply pick back up where we left off."

Baldur suddenly laughed. "Kenna, we never left *off*. We have been doing this dance the whole time. It is time to be honest and accept we are destined to love one another, for good or ill. It is you and me, raven, come what may. It always has been."

Honesty was a painful thing.

"But what if—what if this was not the dragon?" she whispered, the years of uncertainty heavy upon her. "What if your dragon is still coming? Is it over, Baldur? Or is it beginning again?"

He took his time in answering. "I do not know," he finally confessed. "Do I have years? Or only moments? But this I do know—if this moment is to be my last, I will make it a moment that cannot be forgotten. Will you not live in this moment—with me—even if it is to be our last?"

Snow landed on his head, and Baldur glanced up to see the cause. Tosk froze mid-step, apparently moving in closer for a better view. Baldur snatched up a handful of snow and twisted his torso, packing the snow as he turned. Tosk squeaked as the ball sailed toward him. He latched all four paws around the branch, the snow flying within inches of him.

Kenna choked on a laugh, on a sob. Tosk screeched at them, but Baldur turned back to her, his expression charged and determined. He reached out to cup her chin in one of his large hands, a hand roughened with dried dragon's blood. "Ignore him," he ordered. He leaned closer so that she could not avoid his eyes. They were dark, and they were human, and so beautiful. "I meant what I said before. I would rather die a thousand deaths than live without you," he whispered, his rough fingers stroking her jaw even as he held it captive. His gaze traveled the length of her face before returning to her eyes. "I love you, Kenna. I care not what you look like—or how old you may grow—or what you may do or say. I love you as you are. In this moment. Come what may."

Tears sprang to her eyes. "How can you say that?" she whispered.

"Because I could not appreciate you before." He smiled at her, a sad but sweet smile that wormed its way straight into the dark lump that had become her heart. "And now I think I can, because now I know what loss is. Loss is life without you, and I would not choose that. Not for a hundred girls. Or a thousand dragon slayers."

Something bittersweet blossomed to life at the center of the darkness inside her. She felt as if the darkness melted away and something bright began to grow in its stead. "I hated them," she confessed, in a whisper. "Every last one of them."

Baldur laughed and leaned his forehead against hers. "I know."

Baldur and Kenna were kissing in the snow bank, blind to the storm moving in, to the heavy flakes shaking free of the cloud cover. Tosk covered his eyes with his paws, but then slid his fingers apart for another peek. Baldur had his hands full of inky black hair while Kenna, for the first time in her life, was not making a ruckus.

He had to admit he had done quite well with them. It had been a long journey, keeping these two sane, prodding them in the right direction. They had not made it easy on him, especially that raven girl and her ever-biting beak. He rubbed a sore spot on his head, grimacing.

He felt a moment's unease and wondered if he deserved the pecking. After all, it had been his cajoling in the beginning that started this disastrous ordeal. It had also been his idea to start the rumors about the imaginary treasure, to make the village girls more eager to help. That had not worked out so very well, either. Tosk tugged at his ear tufts and squirmed. At last he gave himself a vigorous shake. His being responsible for any of it was really such a *remote* possibility that it was not worth fretting over.

Now that he had settled that worrisome thing, he noticed the rumble in his stomach reminding him that he had been remiss in his usual routines. The dragon, despite his best attempts, had not managed to burn *all* of Tosk's secret stashes. A good thing too because Baldur and Kenna were going to need sustenance in the near future, and it would be up to Tosk to take care of them as usual. He really was quite fond of the prince, despite his unusual taste in girls, and Kenna was growing on him.

The pair would be lost without him.

He turned and pranced across the limb, his muscles tightening as he prepared to leap into the air. Even with the storm moving in and the fortress burning, he felt happy. Things had finally turned around for the good. And, oh, what a tale it would be! But stashes first.

By the bones, he was famished.

As he hurtled through the trees, back toward the fortress, he caught sight of a squat form trundling through the snow. A striped tail bobbed back and forth as the coon waddled away from him.

He might have time to make a quick detour. The coon family that lived in the hollow beneath the oak tree—they were always in the mood for a good story. They were hardly the respectable sort, burglars and scoundrels all, but what did that matter when a there was a tale that needed telling?

So he changed directions and scampered after the raccoon. His stomach protested with another well-timed growl, but he shushed it. He had a tale to tell about his harrowing encounter with the gold-thief—the fire-breather. He must not forget the part where he, the Ever Brave, challenged the dragon single-handed in order to save Baldur from certain scorching.

Well, it would have happened that way if he had not been delayed. Even so, that stupid dragon girl had been right about one thing—this whole episode with the dragon was going to make one glorious tale.

Coming Soon

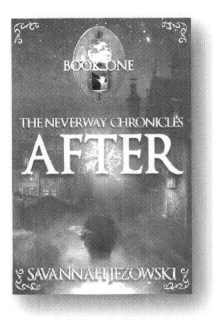

"Some people might say that there are worse fates than death. In some worlds, perhaps that may well be the case. But in mine it would be a lie—there is no greater horror than that which comes after death."

On the streets of an ancient city, with creepers wandering at will and a mysterious assassin leaving corpses all over Pandorum, a young Spook with a dark secret will do anything to keep his brothers safe, even from forces that threaten to tear them apart from within. While others are searching for impossible cures from outlawed Spinners, Conrad Ellis III does not believe in fairy tales and miracles. But when he discovers a strange girl hunted by the assassin, Eli is forced to leave the streets he loves and travel into the very heart of Pandorum to save not only his family but also his city. With his health failing and the danger escalating, he will have no choice but to confront the darkest corners of his soul.

Because if he fails—if his secret is discovered—his life will not be the only one forfeited.

AUTHORS NOTE

Stories have never been just stories to me. Even the most fantastical adventures have elements of truth to them—glimpses of reality. *When Ravens Fall* is some of the truest writing I have ever done, and it is entirely fantasy. All of the characters are make believe—the setting inspired by myths and legends—the plot fashioned around a fairytale. What made it real to me wasn't the story itself but what the story came to mean to me.

I wrote this little tale for someone special to me who loves squirrels. The legend of Ratatoskr, the gossiping squirrel from Norse mythology, was impossible to resist. I fell in love with him before I even began writing him. But what began as a simple story about a mischievous forest critter turned into a study of human nature—specifically, how we respond to the tragedies in our lives.

Each of the characters in this story respond in a different way. Some walk away because they cannot stand to face the potential loss. Others do the unthinkable to change their destiny. Some become bitter. Some become monstrous. Some despair. Others give everything they have, trying to move heaven and earth to make a difference. Some don't know what to think—the idea of someone else's pain is awkward and unsettling. In my own life, I have found myself wanting to follow many of these paths. Instead of being thankful for the time I do have, I want to become bitter for the time I don't. I have felt awkward with other people's pain, I have felt desperate, and I have felt abandoned. I've watched those I love suffer a pain ten times my own and been unable to help. This, I think, is often the most difficult pain to endure.

When Ravens Fall is also a story of restoration. Relationships are never easy. They do not just happen—they require time and work. I wanted to explore some difficult relationships and play with the contrasts between them. In my story, there are two main character struggles that end up being resolved in different ways. One ends happily with the problems being resolved while the other does not. Not all problems will have an easy solution—sometimes the only thing to do is walk away from a toxic environment rather than letting it poison you. Sometimes, healing comes from mending fences, and others times it can only come by letting go.

The thing about pain is that it serves a purpose. If we lose sight of the big picture, we easily fall into bitterness and despair. One of my favorite Bible passages comes from Ecclesiastes 3, a passage that deals with time and purpose. Life cannot be only joy and laughter; it must have its darkness, also. We cannot have day without night, summer without winter, or harvest without rain. Our pain does serve a purpose. We never know when our loss may give someone else hope, courage and strength for their own trials. We do not get to choose the Trials given to us, but we do get to choose what we do with them—how we live them—what we do with the moments that are given to us.

If you take anything from this tale, I sincerely wish you to take Hope—hope that today might become endurable, hope that tomorrow might become better, hope that you might find the strength to see rainbows in spite of the storms raging in your life. I hope you can find the strength to admire the frost on your windshield or the sound of little feet romping through your once tidy rooms. I hope you'll take time to hold your loved ones and thank God for them, even on the bad days. I hope you'll make the most of every moment, that you will do more than just endure—that you will truly live and be content with the dragons in your life.

I hope your dragons take you places you have never imagined.

> *"I know that whatever God does,*
> *It shall be forever.*
> *Nothing can be added to it,*
> *And nothing taken from it.*
> *God does it, that men should fear before Him.*
> *That which is has already been,*
> *And what is to be has already been;*
> *And God requires an account of what is past."*

Ecclesiastes 3:14-15 NKJV

29893633R00079

Made in the USA
Middletown, DE
06 March 2016